und Andere, Esop

Select Fables of Esop and Other Fabulists.

In Three Books

und Andere, Esop

Select Fables of Esop and Other Fabulists.
In Three Books

ISBN/EAN: 9783744792233

Printed in Europe, USA, Canada, Australia, Japan

Cover: Foto ©Andreas Hilbeck / pixelio.de

More available books at **www.hansebooks.com**

SELECT FABLES

OF

ESOP

AND

OTHER FABULISTS.

IN THREE BOOKS.

——*Is not the earth*
With various living creatures, and the air
Repleniſhed, and all theſe at thy command
To come and play before thee? Knoweſt thou not
Their language and their ways? They alſo know,
And reaſon not contemptibly: with theſe
Find paſtime.   Paradiſe Loſt, B. 8. l. 370.

BIRMINGHAM,
Printed by JOHN BASKERVLLE, for
R. and J. DODSLEY in Pall-mall. 1764.

THE
PREFACE.

THE fables of Esop have always been esteemed the best lessons for youth, as being well adapted to convey the most useful maxims, in a very agreeable manner. Accordingly, many writers both in verse and prose, have endeavoured to clothe them in an English dress. It would ill become the Author of this work to animadvert upon their labours: but he thinks it may be said with truth, and he also hopes with modesty, that nothing of this kind, which has been published in prose, can justly discourage him from the present undertaking.

In forming this collection, he has endeavoured to distinguish, by two separate books, the respective compositions of

 the

the earlier and later mythologists; and he trusts it will not be found that he has often been mistaken in this distribution, though an error of that kind might perhaps appear of no great importance. His principal aim was to select such Fables *as would make the strongest and most useful impressions on the minds of youth; and then to offer them in such unaffected language, as might have some tendency to improve their style. If in this he should be allowed to have at all succeeded; the work, it is presumed, will not be unserviceable to young readers, nor wholly unentertaining to persons of maturer judgment.*

To these he has ventured to add a third Book *consisting entirely of original* Fables; *and he offers it to the public with all the diffidence which ought to accompany every modern production, when it appears*

pears

pears in conjunction with writings of established reputation. Indeed, whatever hopes
he has, that the present work may be
favourably received, arise chiefly from
the consideration, that he has been af-
sisted in it by gentlemen of the most distin-
guished abilities; and that several, both
of the old and new Fables, are not written by himself, but by authors, with whom
it is an honour to be connected; and who
having condescended to favour him with
their assistance, have given him an opportunity of making some attonement for
his own defects.

The life of Esop prefixed to this collection, is taken from Monf. de Meziriac, a very learned and ingenious
Frenchman; who being disgusted with
the grofs forgeries of that lying monk
Planudes, published in 1632, the best
account he could collect from ancient

writers of good authority. But this little book, soon after became so extremely scarce, that Monſ. Bayle, *in the firſt edition of his dictionary, laments he never could get a ſight of it;* Dr. Bentley *in his diſ-ſertation on* Eſop's Fables *makes much the ſame complaint; nor does it appear that* Sir Roger Leſtrange *or* Dr. Crox-al, *ever ſo much as heard of* Meziriac's *name. The work indeed in the original has continued equally ſcarce to this day; but an* Engliſh *tranſlation of it falling into the writer's hands, he hath endea-voured in ſome meaſure to correct the lan-guage; adding notes from ſeveral au-thors, particularly from* Boyle's *and* Bentley's *controverſy on the ſubject; and he is perſuaded that the judicious reader will not condemn him for adopting it, inſtead of the fictitious and abſurd rela-tion of* Planudes.

THE
LIFE of ESOP,
COLLECTED FROM
ANCIENT WRITERS.

By Monf. DE MEZIRIAC.

Tranflated into ENGLISH.

WITH NOTES.

THE
LIFE of ESOP.

CHAP. I.

Of the place of his birth.

IT happened to Homer, the prince of Grecian poets, that the place of his nativity was never certainly known; and it would be as difficult to afcertain the country which gave birth to Efop, fo much have ancient authors differed alfo upon this fubject. Some have thought him a [1] Lydian, born in the city of Sardis, the capital of that kingdom; others have believed he drew his origin from the ifland of [2] Samos. Some have maintained that he was a [3] Thracian, of the city of Mefembria: but [4] authors are now, for the moft part, agreed, that he was a native of Phrygia, either of [5] Amorium, or [6] Cotiæum, both towns in the fame province. However, as it may be allowable to conjecture on a point fo dubious, I imagine they who have thought him a Lydian, or a Sa-

mian,

mian, have grounded their opinion on the probability of his being born in one of these places where he spent the greatest part of his life; and 'tis certain, that during his slavery, his common habitation was in the island of 7 Samos; and after he was made free, he lived almost wholly in the court of Crœsus king of Lydia. But though this opinion is not totally destitute of a plausible appearance, the probability of his being a 8 Phrygian, as it is founded on the common consent of many ancient writers, and supported by the most credible authority, is now generally received and established.

N O T E S.

1 *Maximus Tyrius, Differt.* XX. 2 *Suidas.* 3 *The Scholiaft on Ariftophanes. Heraclides in Gronov. Thef. Græc. Tom.* VI. *p.* 2827. 4 *Maximus Tyrius. Differt.* XXXIII. *Lucian's True Hiftory, Book* II. *Stobaeus. Suidas. A. Gellius. Phaedrus.* 5 *Planudes.* 6 *Suidas. Fabricius.* 7 *Jadmon at leaft, his laft Mafter, was of this ifland. Suidas fays expreffly, that Xanthus was a Lydian. Fabricius indeed calls him a Samian, but quotes no authority for it, nor can I find any.* 8 *Phrygia is a province of Afia Minor.*

It may perhaps be acceptable to some readers, and not improper in this place, to add a passage from the learned Mr. Sale, in his notes to the Koran, concerning the Eastern fabulist Lokman, who has been imagined by some writers to be the same person with our Esop. The Arabian writers, says he, affirm that Lokman was the son of Bauvan, who was the son or grandson of a sister or aunt of Job; and that he lived several centuries, even to the time of David, with whom he was conversant in Palestine. According to the description they give of his person, he must have been deformed enough; for they say he was of a black complexion, (whence some call him an Ethiopian) with thick lips, and splay feet: but in return, he received from God, wisdom and eloquence, in a great degree; which, some pretend, were given him in a vision, on his making choice of wisdom preferable to the gift of prophecy, either of which were offered him. The generality of the Mohammedans therefore hold him to have been no prophet, but only a wise man. As to his condition, they say he was a slave, but obtaining his liberty on the following occasion. His Master having one day given him a bitter melon to eat, he paid him such exact obedience as to eat it all; at which his master being surprised, asked him, How he could eat so bitter a fruit? To which he replied, It was no wonder, that he should for once accept a bitter fruit from the same hand from which he had received so many favours. The commentators mention several quick re-

partees

partees of Lokman, which, together with the circum-
stances above mentioned, agree so well with what Maxi-
mus Planudes had written of Esop, that from thence,
and from the fables attributed to Lokman by the Ori-
entals, the last has been generally thought to be no other
*than the Esop of the Greeks.   However that be, (for **I***
*think the matter will bear a dispute) **I** am of opinion*
that Planudes borrowed great part of his life of Esop,
from the tradition he met with in the East concerning
Lokman, concluding them to have been the same person,
because they were both slaves, and supposed to be the wri-
ters of those fables which go under their respective names,
and bear a great resemblance to one another; for it has
long been observed by learned men, that the greater part
of that monk's performance is an absurd romance, and
supported by no evidence of ancient writers.

Sale's Koran. p. 335.

A collection of Lokman's fables may be found in Er-
penius's Arabic Grammar, between thirty and forty in
number, printed in Arabic, with a Latin translation.
They very much resemble the fables of Esop, and have
most of them been inserted in our collections: particu-
larly, the Stag drinking—The old Man and Death—
The Hare and the Tortoise—The Sun and the Wind
—with many others, all of which are in Erpenius's col-
lection, under the name of Lokman. The fables of Pil-

pay,

pay, the other *Eaſtern,* are of quite a different caſt, long, tedious, and frequently interwoven one with another. I have inſerted in this collection, only one fable from *Pilpay, The* Falcon *and the* Hen, in the ſecond book.

CHAP. II.

Of his person, talents, and disposition.

'TIS allowed by all, that Esop was a slave from his youth, and that in this condition, he served several masters: but I am ignorant where Planudes has authority for asserting that he was the most deformed of all men living, exactly resembling Homer's Thersites; I find no ¹ ancient author who thus describes him. What Planudes adds, that the word Esop signifies the same with AEthiop, and was given him on account of the blackness of his visage, may be very justly contradicted: for though some grammarians are of opinion, that from the verb *aetho*, which signifies to scorch, and from the noun *ops*, which signifies visage, the word AEthiop may be formed; yet we learn from Eustathius, that *aetho* (in the future *aeso*) signifies to shine, as well as to burn; and that *ops* with an *o* long signifies the eye: so that the name Esop signifies a man with sparkling eyes. Neither do I give

credit

credit to the same author, when he says, that
Esop had such an impediment in his tongue,
that he could scarcely utter articulate sounds;
as he seems to have attributed this imper-
fection to him, only to have some ground
for the fabulous account which he afterwards gives, of Fortune's appearing to him
in a dream, and bestowing on him the gift
of speech. Altogether as void of probability
is the story which Apollonius tells in [2] Phi-
lostratus; that Mercury, having distributed
to other persons the knowledge of all the
sciences, had nothing left for Esop but the
art of making fables, with which he endowed him. But a principal reason which
prevents me from assenting to what Planudes advances, is, that it cannot be supported
by authority from any [3] ancient author: on
the contrary, 'tis asserted in a Greek frag-
ment of his life, found in the works of Aph-
thonius, that Esop had an excellent disposition, and universal talents; in particular,
a great inclination and aptitude for music;
which is not very consistent with his having a bad voice, and being dumb.

N O T E S.

to his memory: but had he been such a monster as Pla-nudes has made of him, a statue had been no better, than a monument of his ugliness; it had been kinder to his memory to let that alone. The Greeks have several pro-verbs about persons deformed; our Esop, if so very ugly, had been in the first rank of them, especially when his statue stood there, to put every body in mind of it. He was a great favourite of Cræsus king of Lydia; who em-ployed him as his ambassador to Corinth and Delphi: but would such a monster as Planudes has set out, be a fit companion for a prince? or a proper ambassador? I wish I could do that justice to the memory of Esop, as to oblige the painters to change their pencil; for 'tis certain he was no deformed person, and 'tis probable he was very handsome.

Bentley on Esop's Fables.

In answer to all this, Mr. Boyle cites a passage from Eustathius, an author who wrote two hundred years be-fore Planudes was born, which he thinks is evidently built on a supposition that Esop was ugly, and implies that that opinion was common in Eustathius's time. He further tells us, that Lucian, in his True History, says, they used Esop in the Fortunate Islands for a buffoon, or jester, one that made them sport: meaning, I suppose, that he did it as well by his person and outside, as by his ingenious and divertive fables; and, indeed, rather by the first than the latter, as his fables of themselves,

though

though they entertain and please us extremely, do not give us that sort of pleasure that causes laughter; but nothing is so divertive, or raises laughter so much as deformity, especially when wit goes along with it.   We may observe, that when Homer has a mind to excite this light passion in his serious poem, he does it by the means of an ugly man, and an ugly god, Thersites and Vulcan.——But Dr. Bentley's conduct with regard to Esop, is very odd.   He is extremely concerned to have him thought handsome, at the time that he is endeavouring all he can to prove him no author.   He hopes by his civilites to his person, to attone for the injuries which he does him in his writings: which is just such a compliment to Esop's memory, as it would be to Sir William Davenant's, should a man, in defiance of common fame, pretend to make out, that he had always a good nose on his face; but however, he did not write Gondibert.

Boyle against Bentley.

I shall here leave the reader to consider the opinion of these two gentlemen, and to take that which seemeth to him the most probable: only observing, that Mr. Alsop, though a writer at that time in favour of Boyle on the general subject of Esop's Fables, yet, when he afterwards published a collection of those Fables, thought proper to make Esop in the frontispiece, a very handsome person.

C H A P. III.

Of his condition, and the course of his studies.

ESOP's first master, as may be gathered
from the before mentioned Aphthoni-
us, was Zemarchus, or Demarchus, sur-
named Carefias, a native and inhabitant of
Athens: and his passing some part of his
youth in this famous city, the mother and
nurse of science and polite learning, was of
no small advantage to him. 'Tis probable also, that his master, perceiving in him a good
understanding, agreeable manners, lively
genius, and a general capacity; and finding
also that he served him with much affection
and fidelity; 'tis probable, I say, that he
might take care to get him instructed. It
was from Athens then, as from the fountain head, that he drew the purity of the
Greek language. It was there too, that he
acquired the knowledge of moral philosophy, which at that time was the fashionable study; there being but few persons who
made profession of the speculative sciences,

as may be concluded by the seven sages of Greece, the most celebrated men of that age, amongst whom Thales, the Milesian, alone had the curiosity to inquire into the secrets of natural philosophy, and into the subtilties of mathematical learning: The rest were not reputed wise for any other reason, than their publishing certain grave and moral sentences, the truth of which they established, and rendered of some authority, by their prudent and virtuous lives. Esop, indeed, did not follow their method; he wisely considered, that the meanness of his birth, and his servile condition, would not permit him to speak with sufficient authority in the way of sentence and precept; he therefore composed fables, which by a narration pleasing and full of novelty, so charms the minds, even of the most ignorant, that through the pleasure which they receive from it, they *taste* imperceptibly the moral sense which lies concealed underneath.

I know very well that Esop was not the first inventor of those fables, in which the

use

ufe of fpeech is given to animals. The honour of this invention, as [2] Quintilian al-
ledges, is juftly due to the poet Hefiod, who
in the firft book of his Works and Days,
relates very prettily the fable of the [3] hawk
and the nightingale. Be this as it may——
Efop has advanced fo far before every com-
petitor, that all fables of this kind are called
Efopic, becaufe a great number of them are
of his compofing; and the choiceft precepts
of moral philofophy, are by his means, conveyed to us in this agreeable manner. And
indeed, I very highly approve the opinion
of Apollonius, who maintains that the fables of Efop are much more ufeful for the
inftruction of youth, than the fables of the
poets: and his reafons for this affertion are
very pertinent, as may be feen in Philoftra-
tus. But that Efop compofed all his fables
during the time that he was a flave at Athens,
I will not however affirm: I only think it
probable, that it was there he firft became
enamoured of morality, and laid the plan
of teaching the moft beautiful and ufeful
maxims of philofophy, under the veil of
                                    fables:

fables: which neverthelefs he might not publifh till long afterwards, when he had obtained his freedom, had acquired the reputation of being one of the wifeft and ableft men of Greece, and was arrived to great efteem, not only among the common people, but even with princes and kings.

NOTES.

[1] *Whatever honour may arife from being the inventor of this kind of fable, it feems neither to be due to Hefiod, nor to Efop; as Jotham's fable of the trees is certainly more ancient than either of them: and it is for that reafon, placed at the head of this collection.*

[2] *Book* v. *chap.* 11.

[3] *The faid fable is thus rendered by Cooke.*

Whilft now my fable from the birds I bring,
To the great rulers of the earth I fing.
High in the clouds a mighty bird of prey
Bore a melodious nightingale away;
And to the captive, fhivering in defpair,
Thus, cruel, fpoke the tyrant of the air,

Why

Why mourns the wretch in my superior power?
Thy voice avails not in the ravish'd hour;
Vain are thy cries: at my despotic will,
Or I can set thee free: or I can kill.
Unwisely who provokes his abler foe,
Conquest still flies him, and he strives for woe.
Cook's Hesiod, B. I.

C H A P.

C H A P. IV.

Of his different masters, and of his fellow servant, the famous courtezan, Rhodopis.

LET us now resume the thread of our narration. In process of time, Esop was sold to Xanthus, a native of the island of [1] Samos; and after he had served him for a certain time, he was again disposed of to the [2] philosopher Idmon or Jadmon, who was likewise of that country; and had at the same time for his slave, that [3] Rhodopis, who was afterwards so famous as a courtezan. This woman was endowed with very extraordinary beauty, and happening to be carried into Egypt, Charaxus, the brother of Sappho, the poetess, fell so deeply in love with her, that he sold all he had, and reduced himself to extreme poverty, in order to redeem and set her at liberty. She afterwards rose to such eminence in her vocation, and amassed such heaps of wealth, that of the tythe of her gain, she caused great numbers of large [4] spits of iron to be

made,

made, which she sent as an offering to the temple of Apollo at Delphi. And if we may credit certain authors, she amassed such immense treasure, as enabled her to build one of the celebrated [5] pyramids of Egypt. So much, by the way, of this famous courtezan, who was fellow servant with Esop while he lived with Jadmon; to shew how these two persons born, in a servile condition, arrived by very different methods to a more splendid fortune; the one by his merit and the beauties of his mind, the other by the infamous traffic of her personal charms.

For the rest, 'tis certain that it was Jadmon who gave Esop his liberty; whether as a reward for his faithful services, or that he was ashamed to keep longer in servitude a person whose superior qualities rendered him more worthy to command, may be difficult to determine: but the fact is to be proved, by the implied testimony of the scholiast of Aristophanes, on the comedy of the Birds, as well as by the authority of Herodotus

and

and Plutarch; for it follows by neceffary confequence from what they fay, as I fhall fhew particularly when I come to fpeak of the death of Efop. Planudes therefore deferves no credit, when he affirms that Xanthus was the laft mafter of Efop, and the perfon who gave him his liberty. Very little alfo muft be believed of what he relates concerning Efop while he was in the fervice of Xanthus, as he makes him fay and do fo many impertinent and ridiculous things, that none can receive them for true, without imagining Efop an idle buffoon, rather than a ferious Philofopher. And in fine, fince nothing of this ridiculous ftuff is to be found in ancient writers, I think one may with juftice affirm, that they are no better than idle tales, and mere [6] fooleries.

N O T E S.

[1] *The Sholiaft on Ariftophanes, on which Meziriac builds his authority for this, does not fay fo.*

[2] *Neither Herodotus, nor Plutarch, nor Suidas, call him a philofopher: it was a title unknown in the time*
of

CHAP. V

Of his advancement to the court of Crœsus king of Lydia, and of his meeting the seven sages there.

WHATEVER may be doubtful in the life of Esop, there is nothing more certain, than, that after recovering his liberty, he soon acquired a very great reputation amongst the Greeks, being held in almost equal estimation with any of the seven sages, who flourished at this time, that is, the [1] fifty-second olympiad. The fame of his wisdom reaching the ears of Crœsus, that monarch sent for him to his court, admitted him to his friendship, and so obliged him by his favours, that he [2] engaged himself in his service to the end of his days. His residence in the court of this mighty king, rendered him more polite than most of the other philosophers of his time; more complaisant to the humour of princes, and more reconciled to monarchical government, of which he gave evident proofs on divers occasions. For instance; when Crœsus had

prevailed

prevailed with the seven sages to meet in his capital city of Sardis; after having shewn them the magnificence of his court, and his vast riches, he asked them, whom they thought the happiest man of all they had known: Some named one person, and some another? Solon, in particular, gave this praise to 3 Tellus, an Athenian; and also to 4 Cleobis and Biton, Argians, concluding, that no one could be pronounced happy before his death. Esop, perceiving the king was not well satisfied with any of their answers, spoke in his turn, and said—For my part, I am persuaded that Crœsus hath as much pre-eminence in happiness over all other men, as the sea hath over all the rivers. The king was so pleased with this judgment, that he eagerly pronounced that sentence, which has continued ever since a common proverb—*The Phrygian has hit the mark!* When Solon, therefore, took leave of Crœsus, who dismissed him very coolly; Esop being sorry that Solon had spoken to the king with so little complaisance, said to him, as he accompanied him part of the way, O Solon,

Solon, either we muſt not ſpeak to kings, or we muſt ſay what pleaſes them. On the contrary, anſwered Solon, we muſt either not ſpeak to kings at all, or we muſt give them good and uſeful advice. Another time, as Eſop was travelling over Greece, either to ſatisfy his curioſity, or about the particular affairs of Crœſus, it happened that he paſſed through Athens, juſt after ⁵ Piſiſtratus had uſurped the ſovereign power, and aboliſhed the popular ſtate: ſeeing that the Athenians bore the yoke very impatiently, longing to recover their liberty, and to rid themſelves of Piſiſtratus, though his government was eaſy and moderate, Eſop related to them the fable of the frogs that intreated Jupiter to give them a king; exhorted them to ſubmit chearfully to ſo good a prince as Piſiſtratus, leſt in changing they ſhould fall under the power of ſome miſchievous and cruel tyrant.

NOTES.

NOTES.

1 *Laertius, in the life of Chilon.*

2 *Suidas.*

3 *Tellus was a poor Athenian, but a man of great probity; who, upon account of having given his children a good education, and lost his own life in the field of battle, fighting for his country, had this noble testimony given to his happiness, by Solon.*
Plutarch. Diog. Laertius.

4 *Cleobis and Biton were sons to the priestess of Juno, who, when their mother wanted horses for her chariot, set their shoulders to it, and drew it to the temple, which was 48 furlongs. The old lady, being much affected with this instance of filial duty, prayed the goddess Juno to favour them with the greatest blessing that could be bestowed upon mankind: the next morning they were both found dead in the temple. Herod. B. I. Val. Max. B. V. And the story is mentioned also by Cicero in his Tusculan Questions, to shew, that death is to be looked upon rather as an advantage than an evil.*

5 *Phaedrus.*

CHAP.

CHAP. VI.

Some detached particulars of his life, and the improba-
bility of Planudes's account of his travels into Egypt
and Babylon.

THERE are not many other particulars
found concerning Esop, in authors
worthy of credit; except it be, that he once
again met with the seven sages of Greece, in
the court of [1] Periander, king of Corinth.
However, I dare not affirm whether it was
here, or in some other place, that falling
into discourse with Chilon, who had asked
him, What [2] God was doing? He answered,
that he was humbling high things, and ex-
alting low. Some also relate, that to shew
how the life of man abounds with misery,
and that one pleasure is accompanied with
a thousand pains; Esop was wont to say,
that [3] Prometheus having taken earth to
form a man, had tempered and moistened
it, not with water, but with tears.

I reject as pure falshood and invention,
all that Planudes writes of Esop's travels
into

into Egypt and Babylon, because he intermixes stories altogether incredible; and adds to them certain circumstances, which are repugnant to the truth of history, or which wholly overturn the order of time. I shall content myself with alledging two signal falsities, on which he builds all the rest of his narration. He says, that the king who reigned in Babylon when Esop went thither, was called Lycerus. But who has ever read or heard of such a king? Let the catalogue of all the kings of Babylon, from Nabonasser to Alexander the Great, be examined, and you shall not find one amongst them whose name is at all like Lycerus. On the other hand, by the exactest chronology it will appear, that in Esop's time there could be no other king in Babylon, but Nebuchadnezer, and his father Nebopolasser; since Nebopolasser reigned one and twenty years, and Nebuchadnezer forty three, who died the same year with Esop, being the first of the fifty-fourth olympiad. Neither is it more possible to believe, that Esop went into Egypt in the time of king Nectanebus,

 as

as Planudes afferts; fince this king did not begin to reign till two hundred years after the death of Efop: that is to fay, in the hundred and fourth olympiad. And one need not be very learned in chronology, to be certain, that Efop lived partly under the reign of Apries, and partly under that of his Succeffor Amafis, king of Egypt.

N O T E S.

[1] *Plutarch affures* us, *in Convivio Sapientum, that Cræfus fent Efop to Periander the tyrant of Corinth, as well as to the oracle at Delphi: but how does this agree with* Laertius, *who, in the life of Periander, tells us, that according to* Soficrates, *Periander died many years before the reign of Cræfus?*

[2] *Laertius, in the life of Chilon.*

[3] *Themift.* Orat. XXXII.

CHAP. VII.

Of his death.

WHAT Planudes relates about the death of Efop, comes nearer to the truth, than any thing which he has written concerning his life. However, it is ftill fafer to rely on what ancient authors have faid on the fubject; and they record it thus. Efop, being fent by Crœfus to the [1] city of Delphi, with a large fum of gold, in order to offer magnificent facrifices to Apollo, and to diftribute to each citizen four minæ of filver; it happened that [2] differences arofe between him and the townfmen, to fuch a degree, that he fpoke of them in very provoking terms. Among other things, he reproached them with having hardly any arable land, and that were it not for the great concourfe of ftrangers, and the frequent facrifices that were offered in their temple, they would foon be reduced to die of hunger. Not fatisfied with offending them in words, he proceeded to deeds: having per-

formed

formed the facrifices in the manner that Crœfus had ordered, he fent back the reft of the money to the city of Sardis, as judging the Delphians unworthy to partake of the king's liberality. This irritated them againft him to fuch a degree, that they confulted how they might be revenged on him, and confpired by a notorious villany to take away his life. They hid amongft his baggage one of the 3 golden veffels confecrated to Apollo; and as Efop departed towards Phocis, they fent immediate meffengers after him, who fearching his baggage, found the veffel which they themfelves had there depofited. On this, they prefently drag him to prifon, accufe him of facrilege, and fentence him to be precipitated from the rock Hyampia, which was the punifhment commonly inflicted on facrilegious perfons. As they were on the point of throwing him off, in order to deter them from fo execrable an act, by the apprehenfion of divine juftice, which fuffers no wickednefs to go unpunifhed, he told them the 4 fable of the eagle and the beetle. But the Delphians paying

no regard to his fable, pufhed him down
the precipice. It is recorded, however, that
their land was rendered barren, and that
they were afflicted with many ftrange dif-
tempers, for feveral years afterwards. In
this diftrefs they confulted the oracle, and
were anfwered, that all their miferies were
owing to the unjuft condemnation and
death of Efop. On this, they caufed it to
be proclaimed by found of trumpet, at all
the public feafts and general meetings of the
Greeks, that if there were any of the kindred
of Efop, who would demand fatisfaction
for his death, he was defired to come and
exact it of them, in what 5 manner he
pleafed. But no one was found that pretended any right in this affair, till the third
generation; when a Samian prefented himfelf, named Jadmon, grandfon of that
Jadmon, who had been mafter to Efop in the
ifland of Samos: and the Delphians having
made him fome fatisfaction, were delivered
from their calamities. 'Tis faid, that after
this time, they transferred the punifhment
of facrilegious perfons from the rock Hyam-

pia

pia to that of Nauplia. From hence it appears, as I hinted above, to be the opinion of Herodotus and Plutarch, that Jadmon was the laſt maſter of Eſop, and he that ſet him free; becauſe otherwiſe, neither he nor any of his deſcendents could have any intereſt in his death, nor pretend to any right of ſeeking reparation, or receiving ſatisfaction.

NOTES.

[1] *Scholiaſt on Ariſtophanes.* *Vſep.* $\dot{x}$. 1437.

[2] *On what occaſion theſe differences aroſe, we are not expreſsly told: yet ſome circumſtances lead one to imagine, that Eſop's expectations were not quite ſatisfied with regard to the Delphians. From the great concourſe of ſenſible men, who were diſpatched from all parts of Greece to their city; he had probably been led to expect in them ſome ſuperior degree of virtue or wiſdom; but found them, upon a nearer acquaintance, to be not only lazy, but ignorant: his reproaching them for depending ſo much on the benefits ariſing from ſacrifices, as to neglect the cultivation of their lands, ſeems an intimation of the firſt; and his comparing the curioſity that brought him thither, to that of people*

at the sea side, who seeing somewhat come floating to-wards them a great way off at sea, take it at first to be some mighty matter; but upon its driving nearer and nearer to the shore, find it at last to be only a heap of weeds and rubbish—is almost a confirmation of the latter.   Indeed, what authority Sir Roger Lestrange had for making Esop relate this fable to the Delphians, he has not been so kind as to inform us.

3 *Aristophanes.   Heraclides, in Gronov.   Thes. Gracc. Tom.* VI. *p.* 2830.

4 *The eagle and the beetle was one of the most noted fables of* Esop: *Aristophanes mentions it several times. The circumstances of it, as far as they may be col-lected from him, are as follows:* " *That the beetle flew up to heaven; and out of hatred to the eagle, rolled his eggs out of the nest, and so revenged himself of the injury which the eagle had done him.*"   *In* Pace, ℣. 177. *he says,* " *That Esop told this fable to the Delphians, when they had accused him of sacrilege.* Vesp. ℣. 1437. *And when they were about to throw him down the rock," says the Scholiast. The Scholiast upon these passages gives us these farther particulars:* " *It is related in the fables of* Esop, *that the eagle and the beetle were at enmity together, and they destroyed one another's eggs: that the eagle having seized and eaten up the young ones of the beetle, and so given the*

first

first provocation, the beetle got by stealth at the eagle's eggs, and rolled them out of the nest; following him even into the presence of Jupiter: the eagle making his complaint, Jupiter ordered him to make his nest in his lap: while Jupiter had the eggs in his lap, the beetle came flying about him; and Jupiter rising up unawares, to drive the beetle away from his head, threw down the eggs and broke them." Suidas, plainly quoting the same fable, says also, "That he rose up to drive away the beetle flying about his head." Aristophanes in another place uses the proverbal saying, "I will be your midwife, as the beetle was to the eagle." Lysistrata, v. 695. Upon which the Scholiast remarks, "That the beetles destroy the eagles eggs by rolling them out of the nest:" and Suidas says, "That the proverb is used of those, who revenge themselves of such as have first used them ill, though they are much more powerful;" and adds likewise, "That the beetle is said to destroy the eagle's eggs," as a thing that commonly happens.

It is plain from hence, that the fable of the eagle and beetle, as we have it now, differs very much from the original fable of Esop. There is no mention at all of the hare; the provocation given by the eagle, was his destroying the beetle's eggs, or young ones; and the beetle made Jupiter throw the eggs out of his lap, not by throwing a ball of dung into his lap, but by

flying

flying about his head.   What is added in the present fable, of Jupiter's endeavouring to reconcile the two parties, but in vain; and then, to preserve the race of eagles, ordering them to lay their eggs in a season in which no beetles appear; is quite beside Esop's purpose, and the occasion of the fable. The moral, which he intended to express, and which the occassion required, is, agreeable to Suidas's interpretation of the proverb, that the weak often find means to revenge themselves of the powerful, who without provocation have injured them. The latter circumstance relating to the season in which the eagle breeds, is contrary to the observation of the Scholiast on Aristophanes, and Suidas; and, I suppose, is not true in fact.

The genuine fable of Esop is certainly lost: and that which we have may probably have been invented by Planudes; it is in his collection, and stands the fourth in that edition of them, which was printed by Robert Stephens in 1546. That the reader may judge for himself, I will here insert a literal translation of it, given me by the same learned friend, who favoured me with the above observations.

The Eagle and the Beetle.

A Hare being pursued by an Eagle, betook himself for refuge to the nest of the Beetle, whom he intreated to save him. The Beetle therefore interceded with the Eagle, begging of him not to kill the poor suppliant Hare; and conjuring him by the almighty Jupiter, not to slight and disregard his intercession, because he was so small an animal. But the Eagle in great wrath gave the Beetle a flap with his wing, and immediately seized the Hare, and devoured him. When the Eagle flew away, the Beetle flew after him, so far as to learn where his nest was; and then getting to it, rolled down his eggs out of it, and broke them. The Eagle grieved and enraged to think that any one should attempt so audacious a thing, built his nest the next time in a higher place; but the Beetle got to it again, and served him just in the same manner. The Eagle greatly distressed, and not knowing what to do, flew up to Jupiter, (to whom he is accounted sacred) and placed her third brood of eggs as a deposite in the lap of the God, begging him to guard them. Upon this the Beetle, having made a ball of dung, flew up, and dropped it in Jupiter's lap; who rising on a sudden to shake it off, unawares threw down the eggs with it, which were thus again broken. Jupiter being informed by the Beetle, that he had done this to be revenged of the Eagle, who had not only behaved injuriously to him, (the Beetle) but even impiously towards the God himself, told the Eagle when he came to him, that the Beetle was the party aggrieved, and that he complained not without reason: but being unwilling that the race of Eagles should be

diminished,

diminished, he advised the Beetle to come to an accommodation with the Eagle.   As the Beetle would not agree to this, he transferred the Eagle's breeding to another season, when there are no Beetles to be seen.

Absurdities in the forgoing Fable.

The *Hare's flying to the Beetle for protection; or to the Beetle's nest for refuge:——utterly improbable.*

The *Beetle's rolling the Eagle's eggs out of the nest; ——impossible.*

The only moral of the fable is, that no protection, however powerful, shall exempt the oppressive and injurious from the vengeance of the sufferers, however weak.   The circumstance added, that Jupiter transferred the Eagle's breeding to a season when there are no Beetles, destroys this moral; and is probably also false in fact.

3 *Herodotus.   Plutarch.*

C H A P. VIII.

Of the honours done him after his death.

AND now I will readily agree with Planudes, that Efop was regretted by the
greateſt and wifeſt men of Greece, who teſ-
tified to the Delphians how much they re-
fented his death. But I add, that the Athe-
neans, in particular, had Efop in ſo much
honour, that they erected for him a magnificent ſtatue in their city; regarding more
the greatneſs of his perſonal merit, than the
meanneſs of his race and condition. I further ſay, that the opinion which all the
world had conceived of his wiſdom and
probity, encouraged the poets to make the
people believe, that the [1] gods had raiſed him
again to life, as they had done Tyndarus,
Hercules, Glaucus, and Hypolitus. Nay,
ſome have not ſcrupled to affirm, that he
lived many years after his [2] reſurrection, and
fought twice on the ſide of the Greeks, againſt
the Perſians, in the ſtraits of Thermopylæ,
which

which muſt have been above eighty years
after his death.   But theſe are ſuch mani-
feſt abſurdities, as confute themſelves. Neither is it probable, as ſome have aſſerted,
that he wrote [3] two books concerning what
happened to him in the city of Delphi, un-
leſs it be ſuppoſed that he made two voyages
thither, and wrote of the firſt: for in the
laſt, it is very improbable he ſhould have
any time for ſuch a work; neither can it be
grounded on the teſtimony of any author
worthy of credit. 'Tis indeed moſt probable, that he left nothing in writing but
his [4] fables; which, either for the elegance
of the narration, or the uſefulneſs of their
morality, have always been ſo much eſteemed, that many of them have preſerved themſelves in the memories of men for above
two thouſand years. Yet I do not aſſert,
that thoſe which Planudes has publiſhed,
are the [5] very fables which Eſop wrote, as
Planudes has given us too many occaſions
to doubt of his ſincerity; and alſo, as he has
omitted in his collection many fables, which
ancient authors have attributed to Eſop. If

we

we could be certain that it is the genuine work of Esop, we must doubtless confess, that we have no writings in prose more ancient, except the books of Moses, and some others of the Old Testament.

NOTES.

[1] *Scholiast on Aristophanes, Aves, ỳ. 471. Suidas.*

[2] *Ptolomaeus. Hepheftion in Photius et Biblioth.*

[3] *Suidas.*

[4] Dr. *Bentley* asserts, *that it is very uncertain whether Esop left any fables behind him in writing,* to which Mr. *Boyle* answers, *that the phrase of antiquity is the same when they mention any thing of Esop's, as it would have been, had they thought Esop really to have written it: the ancients quote him just as they do other authors.*

Boyle *against* Bentley.

There is a passage in Plato's *Phaedo, where Socrates says, Among the fables of Esop which I had at hand, and knew to be his, I put those into verse that first oc-*

curred

curred to me. Which words imply, that Socrates made use of a written book of Esop's fables.

Ibid.

Of three passages, proceeds the same writer, which the Doctor has brought to prove Esop no author, two of them prove the direct contrary; and the other proves only, that Dr. Bentley has read somebody, that has read Aristophanes. And is this the irresistible evidence, with which he has taken upon him to confront the opinion of two thousand years? Is ti fit that men should make use of their little skill in letters, their conjectures, their fancies, their dreams, to attack the reputation of our first masters in writing? Is it grateful, with such groundless suspicions as these, to fall upon the father of moral fable, whose happy way of conveying knowledge has been ever spoken of with so much respect, and been of such standing use to mankind?

Ibid.

5 *It is remarkable, says father Vavassor, that Henry Stephens, in his Thesaurus Linguae Graecae, never cited Esop's fabes; which shews that he took them for the work of a modern Greek.* It seems probable. nay, almost certain, *says he,* that Planudes collected the fables of Esop, partly from his ancestors, and partly from reading several authors; that some were his own invention, that he added

d

the

the moral and explication, often agreeable to his own fancy, **and that** the whole was put into his own form and words. *He confirms his conjecture by the conformity of style which may be observed between the life of Esop, and the fables: and no one is ignorant that Planudes is the author of that life. Vavassor further observes, that mention is made of the Piraeus in one of Esop's fables. Now the Piraeus was not built till the 76th olympiad; before that time the Phalerum was the port of the Athenians: so that as Esop died in the 54th olympiad, long before Themistocles had built the Piraeus, it would have been the Phalerum, and not the Piraeus, that Esop would have mentioned.*

But father Vavassor is not the first who has taken Planudes for the author of Esop's fables now extant. Nevelet, who published a collection of fables in 1610, declared himself of this opinion. Of all the manuscripts in my possession, *says he,* not one had the fables of Esop which now are published, which I imagine to be written by Planudes, as well as Esop's Life. *The manuscripts he speaks of, were in the library of Heidelberg, and had furnished him with about 136 fables, which he added to those of Esop already printed, which are about 150; so that Nevelet's collection consisted of 286 fables.* Bayle.

The

*The late Dr. Bentley was also of this opinion.   I shall examine, says he, those Greek fables now extant, that assume the name of Esop himself.   There are two parcels of the present fables; the one, which are more ancient, 136 in number, were first published out of the Heidelberg library, by Nevelet in 1610.   The editor himself well observed, that they were falsely ascribed to Esop, because they mention holy monks.   To which I will add, says the Doctor, another remark, that there is a sentence out of Job—*Naked we all came, and naked shall we return.*   But because these two passages are in the epimythion, (the moral) and belong not to the fable itself; they may justly be supposed to be additions only, and interpolations of the true book.   I shall therefore give some better reasons to prove they are a recent work.   That they cannot be Esop's own, the 181st fable is a demonstrative proof: for that is a story of Demades the rhetor, who lived about 200 years after our Phrygians's time.   The 193 is about Momus's carping at the works of the gods.   He there finds this fault in the bull, That his eyes were not placed in his horns, that he might see where he pushed.   But Lucian, speaking of the same fable, has it thus, That his horns were not placed right before his eyes.   And Aristotle has it a third way, That his horns were not placed about his shoulders, where he might make the strongest push; but in the tenderest part, his head.   I think it probable from hence, that Esop did not write a book of*

his

his fables; for then there would not have been such a difference in the telling.——There is great reason to believe they were drawn up by Planudes, a monk of Constantinople, who died in the year 1370: for there is no manuscript, any where, above 300 years old, that has the fables according to that copy.——This ideot of a monk has also given us a book, which he calls a life of Esop, that perhaps cannot be matched in any language, for ignorance and nonsense. He had picked up two or three true stories; that Esop was a slave to one Xanthus, carried a burthen of bread, conversed with Cræsus, and was put to death at Delphi: but the circumstances of these, and all his other tales, are pure invention. He makes Xanthus, an ordinary Lydian, or Samian, to be a philosopher; which word was not heard of in those days, but invented afterwards by Pythagoras. 'Twas the king of Ethiopia's problem to Amasis, king of Egypt, to drink up the fea: *but Planudes makes it a wager of Xanthus with one of his scholars. To say nothing of his chronological errors, mistakes of an hundred or two hundred years, who can read with patience that silly discourse between Xanthus and his man Esop; not a bit better than our penny merriments printed at London bridge.*

Bentley on Esop's fables.

In

*In anfwer to what Dr. Bentley has faid above, con-
cerning the fables of Efop being not written by himfelf,
Mr. Boyle thus argues. Nobody ever imagined that
all, or half the fables, that have gone under the name
of Efop, are his : or that any of them almoft, are in the
very fame words and fyllables, that they were in when
they came out of his hands. They have doubtlefs under-
gone great alterations, fome more and fome lefs; but if
under all thefe changes, ftill the fame little ftory in its
chief circumftances, the fame fimplicity in telling it, the
fame humorous turn of thought, and in a good meafure
the fame words too, have been preferved; there is enough
of Efop left, whereby we may make a true judgment of
his fpirit, and genius, and manner of performance.
When Dr. Bentley fhall clearly have made out, either
that none of thefe fables came from Efop himfelf; or, if
they did, yet that in the very form and caft of them, as
well as the exprefion, they have been fince fo totally al-
tered, that they deferve not to be called the fame; it will
then be time enough to own, that we are unable to judge
of Efop's merit by any thing in the prefent collection : but
till that is done, we may fafely enjoy our opinions, and
they that have admired Efop, may venture to go on,
and admire him ftill.*

*As for what the Doctor has faid of Planudes, I muft
confefs, fays Mr. Boyle, I have not the deepeft venera-
tion for his character; but neither can I think fo defpi-*

 cably

eably of him as the lofty Dr. Bentley does, *because I find him well spoken of by men of good knowledge and judgment, and even* by his adversaries themselves. *Nay,* Dr. Bentley, **I** *think, gives an account of him,* not at all to his *disadvantage, where he says, that the set of fables he put out,* was of his own drawing up: *amongst* which, *there* are several so well turned, *so exactly copyed from nature,* and built on such a true knowledge of human *life and affairs, that 'tis plain he was neither an* ideot *nor* a monk, *that composed them.* But the only reason Dr. *Bentley gives* for his believing *them to be drawn up by Planudes, is, that* there is no manuscript, any where, above 300 years old, that has the fables according to that copy. *No manuscript!* any where! *Very extensive words:* 'tis pretty difficult to answer for all the libraries of *Europe.* But this was an assertion fit to be *laid down by* Dr. Bentley, *because impossible to be proved; and* I believe not difficult to be *disproved:* for, as *much out of the way of these things* as I *live,* I have casually *heard of a manuscript, older* than *Planudes, that* has the *fables according to his* copy; *Vossius's manuscript* I *mean, which, though* I *have not seen it myself, yet better judges than* I *am, who have seen it, assure me, that it is about* 500 *years old, and that Vossius himself always esteemed it so.* 'Tis at *Leyden.*

Boyle against Bentley-

*Fabricius doubts of this manuscript of Vossius men-
tioned by Boyle; it requires, he says, further examina-
tion. Montfaucon promised, (in his Diarium Italicum)
that he would publish from a manuscript of the mona-
stry of St. Mary at Florence, the life of Esop, with
the fables, as they were extant before the time of Planudes, more at large: (in a diffuse style) for that Planudes had omitted some fables, and had written both
the life and the fables in a very different style, and after his own manner.*

Fabricius.

I suppose Montfaucon never fulfilled his promise.

d 4

A N

AN ESSAY ON FABLE.

A N
ESSAY on FABLE.

Introduction.

WHOEVER undertakes to compofe a fable, whether of the fublimer and more complex kind, as the epick and dramatick; or of the lower and more fimple, as what has been called the Efopean; fhould make it his principal intention to illuftrate fome one moral or prudential maxim. To this point the compofition in all its parts muft be directed; and this will lead him to defcribe fome action proper to enforce the maxim he has chofen. In feveral refpects therefore the greater fable and the lefs agree. It is the bufinefs of both to teach fome particular moral, exemplified by an action, and this enlivened by natural incidents. Both alike muft be fupported by appofite and proper characters, and both be furnifhed with fentiments and language fuitable to the character thus employed. I would by no means however infer, that to produce one of thefe fmall pieces requires the fame degree of genius, as to form an epick or dramatick Fable. All I would infinuate, is,

that

that the apologue has a right to fome fhare of our efteem, from the relation it bears to the poems before mentioned: as it is honourable to fpring from a noble ftem, although in ever fo remote a branch. A perfect fable, even of this inferior kind, feems a much ftronger proof of genius than the mere narrative of an event. The latter indeed requires *judgment:* the former, together with judgment, demands an effort of the *imagination.*

Having thus endeavoured to procure thefe little compofitions as much regard as they may fairly claim, I proceed to treat of fome particulars moft effential to their character.

SECT I.

Of the Truth or Moral of a Fable.

'TIS the very effence of a Fable to convey fome *Moral* or *ufeful* Truth, beneath the fhadow of an *allegory.* It is this chiefly that diftinguifhes a *Fable* from a *Tale;* and indeed gives it the pre-eminence in point of ufe and dignity. A Tale may confift of an event either ferious or comic; and, provided it be told agreeably, may be excellent in its *kind,* though it fhould imply no fort of Moral. But the action of a Fable is contrived on *purpofe* to teach and to imprint fome
Truth;

Truth; and fhould clearly and obvioufly include the illuftration of it in the very cataftrophe.

The *Truth* to be preferred on this occafion fhould neither be too obvious, nor trite, nor trivial. Such would ill deferve the pains employed in Fable to convey it. As little alfo fhould it be one that is very dubious, dark, or controverted. It fhould be of fuch a nature, as to challenge the affent of every ingenious and fober judgment; never a point of mere fpeculation; but tending to *inform* or *remind* the reader, of the proper means that lead to happinefs, or at leaft, to the feveral duties, decorums, and proprieties of conduct, which each particular Fable endeavours to enforce.

The reafon why Fable has been fo much efteemed in all ages and in all countries; is perhaps owing to the *polite* manner in which its maxims are conveyed. The very article of giving inftruction fuppofes at leaft, a fuperiority of wifdom in the advifer; a circumftance by no means favourable to the ready admiffion of advice. 'Tis the peculiar excellence of Fable to *wave* this air of fuperiority: it leavs the *reader* to collect the moral; who by thus difcovering more than is fhewn him, finds his principle of felf-love *grati-*

fied,

fied, inftead of being *difgufted*. The attention is either taken off from the advifer; or, if otherwife, we are at leaft flattered by his humility and addrefs.

Befides, inftruction, as conveyed by Fable, does not only lay afide its lofty mien and fupercilious afpect, but appears dreft in all the fmiles and graces which can ftrike the imagination, or engage the paffions. It pleafes in order to convince; and it imprints its moral fo much the deeper, in proportion as it entertains; fo that we may be faid to *feel* our duties at the very inftant we *comprehend* them.

I am very fenfible with what difficulty a Fable is brought to a ftrict agreëment with the foregoing account of it. This however ought to be the writer's *aim*. 'Tis the fimple manner in which the Morals of Efop are interwoven with his Fables, that diftinguifhes him, and gives him the preference to all other mythologifts. His Mountain delivered of a Moufe, produces the Moral of his Fable, in ridicule of pompous pretenders; and his Crow, when fhe drops her cheefe, lets fall, as it were by accident, the ftrongeft admonition againft the power of flattery. There is no need of a feparate fentence to explain it; no
poffibility

poffibility of impreffing it deeper, by that load
we too often fee of accumulated reflections. Indeed the Fable of the Cock and the Precious
Stone is in *this* refpect very exceptionable. The
leffon it inculcates is fo dark and ambiguous, that
different expofitors have given it quite *oppofite* in-
terpretations; fome imputing the Ccok's rejec-
tion of the Diamond to his *wifdom*, and others
to his *ignorance.*

Strictly fpeaking then, one fhould render need-
lefs any *detached* or *explicit* moral. Efop, the father of this kind of writing, difclaimed any fuch
affiftance. 'Tis the province of Fable to give it
birth in the mind of the perfon for whom it is
intended: otherwife the precept is *direct,* which
is contrary to the nature and end of *allegory.* However, in order to give all neceffary affiftance to
young readers, an Index is added to this collection, containing the fubject or moral of each
Fable, to which the reader may occafionally apply.

After all, the *greateft fault* in any compofition
(for I can hardly allow that *name* to riddles) is *obfcurity.* There can be *no* purpofe anfwered by a
work that is unintelligible. Annibal Caracci
and Raphael himfelf, rather than rifque fo un-
pardonable

pardonable a fault, have admitted *verbal explanations* into some of their best pictures. It must be confessed, that every story is not capable of telling its own Moral. In a case of this nature, and this only, it should be *expressly* introduced. Perhaps also, where the point is doubtful, we ought to shew *enough* for the less acute, even at the hazard of shewing *too much* for the more sagacious; who, for this very reason, that they *are* more sagacious, will pardon a superfluity which is such to *them alone*.

But, on these occasions, it has been matter of dispute, whether the moral is better introduced at the end or beginning of a Fable. Esop, as I said before, universally rejected any separate Moral. Those we *now* find at the close of his Fables, were placed there by other hands. Among the ancients, Prædrus; and Gay, among the moderns, inserted theirs at the *beginning*: La Motte prefers them at the *conclusion*; and Fontaine disposes of them *indiscriminately*, at the beginning or end, as he sees convenient. If, amidst the authority of such great names, I might venture to mention my *own* opinion, I should rather *prefix* them as an *introduction*, than *add* them as an *appendage*. For I would neither pay my *reader* nor *myself* so bad a compliment, as to suppose,

after

after he had read the Fable, that he was not able
to difcover its meaning. Befides, when the Moral of a Fable is not very prominent and ftriking,
a leading thought at the beginning puts the
reader in a proper track. He knows the game
which he purfues: and, like a beagle on a warm
fcent, he follows the fport with alacrity, in proportion to his intelligence. On the other hand,
if he has *no* previous intimation of the defign,
he is puzzled throughout the Fable; and cannot
determine upon its merit without the trouble of
a frefh perufal. A ray of light, imparted at firft,
may fhew him the tendency and propriety of
every expreffion as he goes along; but while he
travels in the dark, no wonder if he ftumble or
miftake his way.

SECT. II.

Of the Action and Incidents proper for a Fable.

IN chufing the action or allegory, three conditions are altogether expedient. I. It muft be
clear: that is, it ought to fhew without equivo-
cation, precifely and obvioufly, what we intend
fhould be underftood. II. It muft be *one* and
entire. That is, it muft not be compofed of feparate and independent actions, but muft tend
in all its circumftances to the completion of one
fingle event. III. It muft be *natural;* that is,

e

founded,

founded, if nor on Truth, at leaſt, on Probability; on popular opinion; on that relation and
analogy which things bear to one another, when
we have gratuitouſly endowed them with the human faculties of ſpeech and reaſon.   And theſe
conditions are taken from the nature of the human mind; which cannot endure to be embarraſſed, to be bewildered, or to be deceived.

A Fable offends againſt *preſpicuity,* when it leaves
us doubtful *what* Truth the Fabuliſt intended to
convey. We have a ſtriking example of this in
Dr. Croxall's Fable of the creaking wheel. "A
coachman, ſays he, hearing one of his wheels
creak, was ſurpriſed; but more eſpecially, when
he perceived that it was the worſt wheel of the
whole ſet, and which he thought had but little
pretence to take ſuch a liberty. But, upon his
demanding the reaſon why it did ſo, the wheel
replied, that it was natural for people who labour-
ed under any affliction or calamity to complain."
Who would imagine this Fable deſigned, as the
author informs us, for an admonition to repreſs,
or keep our complaints to *ourſelves,* or if we muſt
let our ſorrows ſpeak, to take care it be done in
ſolitude and retirement. The ſtory of this Fable
is not well imagined: at leaſt, if meant to ſupport
the Moral which the author has drawn from it.

A

A Fable is faulty in refpect to unity; when the feveral circumftances point *different* ways; and do not center, like fo many lines, in one diftinct and unambiguous Moral. An example of this kind is furnifhed by *La Motte* in the obfervation he makes on Fontaine's two pigeons. "Thefe pigeons had a reciprocal affection for each other. One of them fhewing a defire to travel, was earneftly oppofed by his companion, but in vain. The former fets out upon his rambles, and encounters a thoufand unforefeen dangers; while the latter fuffers almoft as much at home, through his apprehenfions for his roving friend. However, our traveller, after many hair-breadth efcapes, returns at length in fafety back, and the two pigeons are, once again, mutually happy in each other's company." Now the application of this Fable is utterly vague and uncertain, for want of circumftances to determine, whether the author defigned principally to reprefent the *dangers* of the *Traveller:* his friend's *anxiety* during his *abfence;* or their *mutual happinefs* on his *return.* Whereas, had the travelling pigeon met with no difafters on his way, but only found all pleafures infiped for want of his friend's participation; and had he returned from no other motive, than a defire of feeing him again, the whole then had happily clofed in this one confpicuous

inference,

inference, that the presence of a real friend is the most desirable of all gratifications.

The last rule I have mentioned, that a Fable should be natural, may be violated several ways. 'Tis opposed, when we make creatures enter into unnatural associations. Thus the sheep or the goat must not be made to hunt with the lion; and it is yet *more* absurd, to represent the lion as falling in love with the forester's daughter. 'Tis infringed, by ascribing to them appetites and passions that are not consistent with their known characters; or else by employing them in such occupations, as are foreign and unsuitable to their respective natures. A fox should not be said to long for grapes; an hedgehog pretend to drive away flies; nor a partridge offer his service to delve in the vineyard. A ponderous iron and an earthen vase should not swim together down a river; and he that should make his goose lay golden eggs, would shew a luxuriant *fancy*, but very little *judgment*. In short, nothing besides the faculty of speech and reason, which Fable has been allowed to confer even upon inanimates, must ever *contradict* the nature of things, or at least, the commonly received opinion concerning them.

Opinious

Opinions indeed, although *erroneous*, if they either *are*, or *have* been univerfally received, may afford fufficient foundation for a Fable. The mandrake, *here*, may be made to utter groans; and the dying fwan, to pour forth her elegy. The fphinx and the phœnix, the fyren and the centaur, have all the exiftence that is requifite for Fable. Nay, the goblin, the fairy. and even the man in the moon, may have each his province allotted him, provided it be not an *improper* one. Here the notoriety of opinion fupplies the place of fact, and in *this manner* truth may fairly be deduced from falfehood.

Concerning the incidents proper for Fable, it is a rule without exception, that they ought always to be *few*; it being foreign to the nature of this compofition to admit of much variety. Yet a Fable with only *one* fingle incident may poffibly appear too naked. If Efop and Phædrus are herein fometimes too fparing, Fontaine and La Motte are as often too profufe. In this, as in moft other matters, a medium certainly is beft. In a word, the incidents fhould not only be few, but fhort; and like thofe in the Fables of "the fwallow and other birds," "the miller and his fon," and "the court and country-moufe," they

    muft

muſt naturally ariſe out of the ſubjeſt, and ſerve to illuſtrate and enforce the Moral.

SECT. III.

Of the Perſons, Charaſters, and Sentiments of Fable.

THE race of animals *firſt* preſent themſelves as the proper aſtors in this little drama. They are indeed a ſpecies that aproaches, in many reſpeſts, ſo near to our own, that we need only lend them *ſpeech*, in order to produce a ſtriking reſemblance. It would however be unreaſonable, to expeſt a ſtriſt and univerſal ſimilitude. There is a certain *meaſure* and *degree* of analogy, with which the moſt diſcerning reader will reſt contented: for inſtance, he will accept the *properties* of animals, although *neceſſary* and *invariable*, as the images of our *inclinations*, tho' never ſo *free*. To require *more* than this, were to ſap the very foundations of allegory; and even to deprive ourſelves of half the pleaſure that flows from poetry in general.

Solomon ſends us to the ant, to learn the wiſdom of induſtry: and our inimitable ethic poet introduces nature herſelf as giving us a *ſimilar* kind of counſel.

Thus

Thus then to Man the voice of Nature spake;
"Go, from the Creatures *thy instructions take—*
*"*There *all the forms of social union find,*
"And thence, *let reason late instruct mankind."*

He suppofes that animals in their *native* characters, *without* the advantages of fpeech and reafon which are defigned them by the Fabulifts, may in regard to *Morals* as well as *Arts*, become examples to the human race. Indeed, I am afraid we have fo far deviated into afcititious appetites and fantaftic manners, as to find the expediency of copying from *them* that fimplicity we ourfelves have loft. If animals in themfelves may be thus exemplary, how much more may they be made inftructive, under the direction of an able Fabulift; who by conferring upon them the gift of language. contrives to make their inftincts more intelligible and their examples more determinate!

But thefe are not his *only* actors. The Fabulift has one advantage above all other writers whatfoever; as all the works both of art and nature are more immediately at his difpofal. He has, in this refpect, a liberty not allowed to epick, or dramatick writers; who are undoubt-

e 4

edly

edly more limited in the choice of perfons to be employed. He has authority to prefs into his fervice every kind of exiftence under heaven: not only beafts, birds, infects, and all the animal creation; but flowers, fhrubs, trees, and all the tribe of vegetables. Even mountains, foffils, minerals, and the inanimate works of nature, difcourfe articulately at his command, and act the part which he affigns them. The virtues, vices, and every *property* of beings, receive from him a *local habitation and a name*. In fhort he may perfonify, beftow life, fpeech and action, on whatever he thinks proper.

It is eafy to imagine what a fource of *novelty* and *variety* this muft open, to a genius capable of receiving, and of employing, thefe ideal perfons in a proper manner; what an opportunity it affords him to diverfify his images, and to treat the fancy with change of *objects;* while he ftrengthens the underftanding, or regulates the paffions, by a fucceffion of *Truths*. To raife beings like thefe into a ftate of action and intelligence, gives the Fabulift an undoubted claim to that *firft* character of the poet, a *Creator*. I rank him not, as I faid before, with the writers of epick or dramatick poems; but the maker of pins or needles is as much an artift, as an anchor-fmith:

fmith: and a painter in miniature may fhew as much fkill, as he who paints in the largeft proportions.

When thefe perfons are once raifed, we muſt carefully injoin them proper tafks; and affign them fentiments and language fuitable to their feveral natures, and refpective properties.

A raven fhould not be extolled for her voice, nor a bear be reprefented with an elegant fhape. 'Twere a very obvious inftance of abfurdity, to paint an hare, cruel; or a wolf, compaffionate. An afs were but ill qualified to be General of an army, though he may well enough ferve perhaps for one of the trumpeters. But fo long as popular opinion allows to the lion, magnanimity; rage, to the tiger; ftrength, to the mule; cunning, to the fox; and buffoonery, to the monkey; why may not they fupport the characters of an Agamemnon, Achilles, Ajax, Ulyffes and Therfites? The truth is, when Moral actions are with judgment attributed to the brute creation. we fcarce *perceive* that nature is at all violated by the Fabulift. He appears, at *moſt*, to have only tranflated their language. His lions, wolves, and foxes, *behave* and *argue* as thofe creatures *would*, had they originally been endowed with the human faculties of speech and reason.

But greater art is yet required, whenever we personify *inanimate* beings. Here the copy so far deviates from the great lines of nature, that, without the nicest care, reason will revolt against the fiction. However, beings of *this* sort, managed ingeniously and with addrefs, recommend the Fabulist's invention by the grace of novelty and of variety. Indeed the analogy between things natural and artificial, animate and inanimate, is often so very striking, that we can, with seeming propriety, give passions and sentiments to every individual part of existence. Appearance favours the deception. The vine may be *enamoured* of the elm; her embraces testify her passion. The swelling mountain may, naturally enough, be *delivered* of a mouse. The gourd may reproach the pine, and the sky-rocket insult the stars. The axe may follicit a new handle of the forest; and the moon, in her *female* character, request a fashionable garment. Here is nothing incongruous; nothing that shocks the reader with impropriety. On the other hand, were the axe to defire a fine perriwig, and the moon petition for a new pair of boots; probability would *then* be violated, and the abfurdity become too glaring.

SECT.

SECT. IV.

On the Language of Fable.

THE moſt beautiful Fables that ever were invented, may be disfigured by the *Language* in which they are clothed.   Of this, poor Eſop, in ſome of his Engliſh dreſſes, affords a melancholy proof.   The ordinary ſtyle of Fable ſhould be *familiar*, but it ſhould alſo be *elegant*.   Were I to inſtance any ſtyle that I ſhould prefer on this occaſion, it ſhould be that of Mr. *Addiſon*'s little tales in the Spectator.   That eaſe and ſimplicity, that conciſeneſs and propriety, that ſubdued and decent humour he ſo remarkably diſcovers in thoſe compoſitions ; ſeem to have qualified him for a Fabuliſt, almoſt beyond any other writer.   But to return.

The *Familiar*, ſays Mr. La Motte, to whoſe ingenious *Eſſay* I have often been obliged in this diſcourſe, is the general tone or accent of Fable. It was thought ſufficient, on its firſt appearance, to lend the animals our moſt common language. Nor indeed have they any extraordinary *pretenſions* to the ſublime ; it being requiſite they ſhould *ſpeak* with the ſame ſimplicity that they *behave*.

The

The *familiar* alfo is more proper for infinua-
tion, than the *elevated;* this being the language
of *reflection,* as the former is the voice of *fentiment.*
We guard ourfelves againft the one, but lie open
to the other; and inftruction will always the
moft effectually fway us, when it appears leaft
jealous of its rights and privileges.

The *familiar* ftyle however that is here required,
notwithftanding that appearance of *Eafe* which
is its character, is perhaps more difficult to write,
than the *elevated* or *fublime.* A writer more readily
perceives when he has rifen above the common
language; than he perceives, in fpeaking this
language, whether he has made the choice that
is moft fuitable to the occafion: and it is neverthelefs, upon *this happy choice* that all the charm
of the *familiar* depends. Moreover, the *elevated*
ftyle deceives and feduces, although it *be not* the
beft chofen; whereas the *familiar* can procure itfelf no fort of refpect, if it be not eafy, natural,
juft, delicate, and unaffected. A Fabulift muft
therefore beftow great attention upon his ftyle:
and even labour it fo much the *more,* that it may
appear to have coft him no pains at all.

The authority of *Fontaine* juftifies this opinion
in regard to ftyle. His Fables are perhaps the
beft

beft examples of the *genteel familiar*, as Sir Roger L'Eftrange affords the groffeft, of the *indelicate* and *low*. When we read that "while the frog and the moufe were difputing it at fword's point, down comes a kite *powdering* upon them in the *interim*, and *gobbets up* both together to part the fray." And where the fox reproaches "a bevy of jolly goffiping wenches making merry over a *dish of pullets*, that, if *he* but peeped into a hen-rooft, they always made a bawling with *their dogs* and *their baftards*; while you yourfelves, fays he, can lie *ftuffing your guts* with your hens and your capons, and not a *word of the pudding*." This *may* be *familiar*, but is alfo *coarfe* and *vulgar*; and cannot fail to difguft a reader that has the leaft degree of tafte or delicacy.

The ftyle of Fable then muft be fimple and familiar; and it muft *likewife* be correct and elegant. By the former, I would advife that it fhould not be loaded with figure and metaphor; that the difpofition of words be natural; the turn of fentences, eafy; and their conftruction, unembarraffed. By elegance, I would exclude all coarfe and provincial terms; all affected and puerile conceits; all obfolete and pedantick phrafes. To this I would adjoin, as the word perhaps implies, a certain finifhing polifh, which gives

a grace and fpirit to the whole; and which, tho'
it have always the *appearance* of nature, is almoft
ever the *effect* of art.

But, notwithftanding all that has been faid,
there are fome occafions on which it is allowable,
and even expedient to change the ftyle. The
language of a Fable muft rife or fall in conformity
to the fubject. A *Lion*, when introduced in his
regal capacity, muft hold difcourfe in a ftrain
fomewhat more elevated than a *Country-Moufe.*
The lionefs then becomes his *Queen*, and the
beafts of the foreft are called his *Subjects:* a method that offers *at once* to the imagination, both
the *animal* and the *perfon* he is defigned to reprefent. Again, the buffoon-monkey fhould avoid
that pomp of phrafe, which the owl employs as
her beft pretence to wifdom. Unlefs the ftyle
be thus judicioufly varied, it will be impoffible
to preferve a juft diftinction of character.

Defcriptions, at once concife and pertinent,
add a grace to Fable; but are *then* moft happy,
when included in the action: whereof the Fable
of *Boreas and the Sun* affords us an example. An
epithet well chofen is often a defcription in *itfelf;*
and fo much the more agreeable, as it the lefs
retards us in our purfuit of the cataftrophe.

I

I might enlarge much further on the fubject, but perhaps I may appear to have been too diffufe already. Let it fuffice to hint, that little *ftrokes of humour*, when arifing naturally from the fubject; and *incidental reflections*, when kept in due fubordination to the principal, add a value to thefe compofitions. Thefe latter however fhould be employed very fparingly, and with great addrefs; be very few and very fhort: It is fcarcely enough that they naturally refult from the fubject: they fhould be fuch as may appear *neceffary* and *effential* parts of the Fable. And when thefe embellifhments, pleafing in *themfelves*, tend to illuftrate the *main action*, they then afford that namelefs grace remarkable in Fontaine and fome few others; and which perfons of the beft difcernment will more eafily *conceive*, than they can *explain*.

R. DODSLEY.

1. The Trees and the Bramble.

2. The Frogs desire a King.

3. The Wolf and Shepherds.

4. The Belly and Limbs.

5. The Fox and Swallow.

6. The Fox and Crow.

7. The Fox and Stork.

8. Daw with borrowed Feathers.

9. The Wolf and Lamb.

10. Mountain in labour.

11. The Boys and Frogs.

12. Lark and her Young.

FABLES.

BOOK I.

FROM THE

ANCIENTS.

B

FABLE I.

The Trees and the Bramble.

THE Ifraelites, ever murmuring and dif-
contented under the reign of Jehovah,
were defirous of having a king, like the
reft of the nations.   They offered the kingdom
to Gideon their deliverer; to him, and to his
pofterity after him: he generoufly refufed their
offer, and reminded them, that Jehovah was
their king.   When Gideon was dead, Abime-
lech, his fon by a concubine, flew all his other
fons to the number of feventy, Joatham alone
efcaping; and by the affiftance of the She-
chemites made himfelf king. Joatham, to repre-

B 2

fent

fent to them their folly, and to fhew them, that the *moft* deferving are generally the *leaft* ambitious, whereas the *worthlefs* grafp at power with eagernefs, and exercife it with infolence and tyranny, fpake to them in the following manner.

Hearken unto *me*, ye men of Shechem, fo may God hearken unto *you*. The Trees, grown weary of the ftate of freedom and equality in which God had placed them, met together to chufe and to anoint a king over them: and they faid to the Olive-tree, Reign *thou* over us. But the Olive-tree faid unto them, Shall I quit my fatnefs wherewith God and man is honoured, to difquiet myfelf with the cares of government, and to rule over the Trees? And they faid unto the Fig-tree, Come *thou*, and reign over us. But the Fig-tree faid unto them, Shall I bid adieu to my fweetnefs and my pleafant fruit; to take upon me the painful charge of royalty, and to be fet over the Trees? Then faid the Trees unto the Vine, Come *thou* and reign over us. But the Vine faid alfo unto them, Shall I leave my wine which honoureth God and cheareth man, to bring upon myfelf nothing but trouble and anxiety, and to become king of the Trees? we are happy in our prefent lot: feek fome other to reign over you. Then faid all the Trees unto the
Bramble,

Bramble, Come *thou* and reign over us. And the Bramble said unto them, I *will* be your king; come ye all under my shadow, and be safe; obey me, and I will grant you my protection. But if you obey me not, out of the Bramble shall come forth a fire, which shall devour even the *cedars of Lebanon.*

F A B L E II.

The Frogs petitioning Jupiter for a King.

AS Esop was travelling over Greece, he happened to pass thro' Athens just after Pisistratus had abolished the popular state, and usurped a sovereign power; when perceiving that the Athenians bore the yoke, tho' mild and easy, with much impatience, he related to them the following fable.

The commonwealth of Frogs, a discontented, variable race, weary of liberty, and fond of change, petitioned Jupiter to grant them a king. The good-natured deity, in order to indulge this their request, with as little mischief to the petitioners as possible, threw them down a *log.* At first they regarded their new monarch with great reverence, and kept from him at a most respectful distance: but perceiving his tame and peaceable

able

able difpofition, they by degrees ventured to approach him with more familiarity, till at length they conceived for him the utmoft contempt. In this difpofition, they renewed their requeft to Jupiter, and intreated him to beftow upon them another king. The Thunderer in his wrath fent them a *crane*, who no fooner took poffeffion of his new dominions, than he began to devour his fubjects one after another in a moft capricious and tyrannical manner. They were now far more diffatisfied than before; when applying to Jupiter a third time, they were difmiffed with this reproof, that the evil they complained of, they had imprudently brought upon themfelves; and that they had no other remedy *now* but to fubmit to it with patience.

FABLE III.

The Wolf and the Shepherds.

HOW apt men are to condemn in others, what they practife themfelves without fcruple!

A Wolf, fays Plutarch. peeping into a hut, where a company of Shepherds where regaling themfelves with a joint of mutton; Lord, faid he, what a clamour would thefe men have raifed, if they had catched me at fuch a banquet!

FABLE

F A B L E IV.

The Belly and the Limbs.

MENENIUS AGRIPPA, a Roman con-
ful, being deputed by the fenate to ap-
peafe a dangerous tumult and fedition of the
people, who refufed to pay the taxes neceffary
for carrying on the bufinefs of the ftate; convinced them of their folly, by delivering to them
the following fable.

My friends and country men, faid he, attend
to my words. It once happened that the members
of the human body, taking fome exceptions at
the conduct of the Belly, refolved no longer to
grant him the ufual fupplies. The Tongue firft,
in a fedtious fpeech, aggravated their grievances;
and after highly extolling the activity and diligence of the Hands and Feet, fet forth how hard
and unreafonable it was, that the fruits of their labour fhould be fquandered away upon the infatiable cravings of a fat and indolent Paunch,
which was entirely ufelefs, and unable to do
any thing towards helping himfelf. This fpeech
was received with unanimous applaufe by all the
Members. Immediately the Hands declared they
would work no more; the Feet determined to

carry

carry no farther the load of Guts with which they had hitherto been oppreſſed; nay, the very Teeth refuſed to prepare a ſingle morſel more for his uſe. In this diſtreſs, the Belly beſought them to conſider maturely, and not foment ſo ſenſelefs a *rebellion.* There is none of you, ſays he, can be ignorant that whatſoever you be-ſtow upon me, is immediately converted to your uſe, and diſperſed by me for the *good of you all* into every Limb. But he remonſtrated in vain; for during the clamours of paſſion, the voice of reaſon is always diſregarded. It being there-fore impoſſible for him to quiet the tumult, he ſtarved for want of their aſſiſtance, and the body waſted away to a ſkeleton. The Limbs, grown weak and languid were ſenſible at laſt of their er-ror, and would fain have returned to their re-ſpective duties; but it was now too late, death had taken poſſeſſion of the whole, and they *all periſhed* together.

FABLE

FABLE V.

*The Fox and the * Swallow.*

ARISTOTLE informs us that the following fable was spoken by Esop to the Samians, on a debate upon changing their ministers. who were accused of plundering the commonwealth.

A Fox swimming across a river, happened to be entangled in some weeds that grew near the bank, from which he was unable to extricate himself. As he lay thus exposed to whole swarms of flies, who were galling him and sucking his blood; a Swallow observing his distress, kindly offered to drive them away. By no means, said the Fox; for if *these* should be chased away, who are already sufficiently gorged, *another* more hungry swarm would succeed, and I should be robbed of every remaining drop of *blood* in my veins.

* *Instead of the Swallow, it was originally a Hedgehog: but as that creature seemed very unfit for the business of driving away flies, it was thought more proper to substitute the Swallow.*

FABLE VI.

The Fox and the Raven.

A Fox obferving a Raven perched on the branch of a tree, with a fine piece of cheefe in her mouth, immediately began to confider how he might poffefs himfelf of fo delicious a morfel. Dear madam, faid he, I am extreamely glad to have the pleafure of feeing you this morning: your beautiful fhape, and fhining feathers, are the delight of my eyes; and would you condefcend to favour me with a fong, I doubt not but your voice is equal to the reft of your accomplifhments. Deluded with this flattering fpeech, the tranfported Raven opened her mouth, in order to give him a fpecimen of her pipe, when down droped the cheefe: which the Fox immediately fnatching up, bore it away in triumph, leaving the Raven to lament her credulous vanity at her leifure.

FABLE VII.

The Fox and the Stork.

THE Fox, tho' in general more inclined to *roguery* than *wit*, had once a ftrong inclination to play the wag with his neighbour the Stork.

Stork. He accordingly invited her to dinner in great form; but when it came upon the table, the Stork found it confifted intirely of different foups, ferved up in broad fhallow difhes. fo that fhe could only dip in the end of her bill, but could not poffibly fatisfy her hunger. The Fox lapped it up very readily, and every now and then, addreffed himfelf to his gueft, defired to know how fhe liked her entertainment; hoped that every thing was feafoned to her mind; and protefted he was very forry to fee her eat fo *fparingly.* The Stork, perceiving fhe was played upon, took no notice, but pretended to like every difh extremely: and at parting preffed the Fox fo earneftly to return her vifit, that he could not in civility refufe. The day arrived, and he repaired to his appointment; but to his great mortification, when dinner appeared, he found it compofed of minced meat, ferved up in long narrow-necked glaffes; fo that he was only tantalized with the *fight* of what it was impoffible for him to *tafte.* The Stork thruft in her long bill, and helped herfelf very plentifully; then turning to Reynard, who was eagerly licking the outfide of a jarr where fome fauce had been fpilled—I am very glad, faid fhe fmiling, that you feem to have fo good an appetite; I hope you will make as hearty a dinner at *my* table as I did the other

day

day at *yours.* Reynard hung down his head, and looked very much difpleafed.—Nay, nay, faid the Stork, don't pretend to be out of humour about the matter: they that cannot *take* a jeft fhould never *make* one.

FABLE VIII.

The Daw with borrowed Feathers.

WHEN a pert young templer, or city apprentice, fets up for a fine gentleman, with the affiftance of an imbroidered waiftcoat and Drefden ruffles, but without *one* qualification proper to the character; how frequently does it happen, that he is laughed at by his equals, and defpifed by thofe whom he prefumed to imitate!

A pragmatical Jackdaw was vain enough to imagine, that he wanted nothing but the coloured plumes, to render him as elegant a bird as the Peacock. Puffed up with this wife conceit, he dreffed himfelf with a fufficient quantity of their moft beautiful feathers, and in this borrowed garb, forfaking his old companions, endeavoured to pafs for a Peacock. But he no fooner attempted to affociate with thefe genteel creatures, than an affected ftrut betrayed the vain
pretender.

pretender. The offended Peacocks, plucking from him their degraded feathers, soon ftriped him of his finery, reduced him to a *mere Jackdaw*, and drove him back to his brethren; by whom he was now equally defpifed, and juftly punifhed with derifion and contempt.

FABLE IX.

The Wolf and the Lamb.

WHEN cruelty and injuftice are armed with power, and determined on oppreffion, the ftrongeft pleas of innocence are preferred in vain.

A Wolf and a Lamb were accidentally quenching their thirft togther at the fame rivulet. The Wolf ftood towards the head of the ftream, and the Lamb at fome diftance below. The injurious beaft, refolved on a quarrel, fiercely demands— How dare you difturb the water which I am drinking? The poor Lamb, all trembling, replies, How, I befeech you, can that *poffibly* be the cafe, fince the current fets from you to me? Difconcerted by the force of truth, he changes the accufation. Six months ago, fays he, you vilely flandered me. Impoffible, returns the Lamb, for I was not then born. No matter, it was your father then, or some of your relations; and immediately seizing the innocent Lamb, he tore him to pieces.

FABLE X.

The Mountain in Labour.

A Rumour once prevailed, that a neighbouring Mountain was in Labour; it was affirmed that she had been heard to utter prodigious groans; and a general expectation had been raised, that some extraordinary birth was at hand. Multitudes flocked with much eagerness to be witnesses of the wonderful event: *one* expecting her to be delivered of a giant; *another* of some enormous monster; and *all* were suspended in earnest expectation of somewhat grand and astonishing. When, after waiting with great impatiance a considerable time, behold!—*out crept a Mouse.*

FABLE XI.

The Boys and the Frogs.

ON the margin of a large lake, which was inhabited by a great number of Frogs, a company of Boys happened to be at play. Their diversion was duck and drake; and whole vollies

of

of ſtones were thrown into the water, to the great annoyance and danger of the poor terrified Frogs. at length one of the moſt hardy, lifting up his head above the furface of the lake; Ah, dear children, faid he, why will ye learn ſo ſoon the cruel practices of your race? Confider, I befeech you, that tho' this may be *ſport* to you, it is *death* to us.

FABLE XII.

The Lark and her Young.

A Lark having built her neſt in a field of corn, it grew ripe before her Young were well able to fly. Apprehenſive for their fafety, ſhe enjoined them, while ſhe went out in order to provide for their fubfiſtence, to liſten very attentively to any difcourfe they might hear about reaping the field. At her return they told her, that the farmer and his fon had been there, and had agreed to fend to fome of their neighbours, to affiſt them in cutting it down the next day. And ſo they depend, it feems, upon *neighbours,* faid the mother: very well: then I think we have no occafion to be afraid of *tomorrow.* The next day ſhe went out, and left them the fame injunction as before. When ſhe returned, they acquainted her that the farmer and his fon had

again

again been there, but as none of their neighbours came to their affistance, they had deferred reaping till the next day, and intended to fend for help to their *friends* and *relations*. I think we may ftill venture another day, fays the mother; but however be careful as before, to let me know what paffes in my abfence. They now inform her, that the farmer and his fon had a *third time* vifited the field; and finding that neither *friends* nor *relations* had regarded their fummons, they were determined to come the next morning and cut it down *themfelves*. Nay, then, replied the Lark, it is time to think of removing: for as they now depend only upon *themfelves* for doing their own bufinefs, it will undoubtedly be performed.

F A B L E XIII.

The Stag drinking.

A Stag quenching his thirft in a clear lake, was ftruck with the beauty of his horns, which he faw reflected in the water. At the fame time, obferving the extreme flendernefs of his legs: What pity it is, faid he, that fo fine a creature fhould be furnifhed with fo defpicable a fet of fpindle fhanks! what a truely noble animal I fhould be, were my legs in any degree an-

fwerable

fwerable to my horns! In the midſt of this foli-
loquy, he was alarmed with the cry of a pack of
hounds. He immediately flies through the foreſt,
and leaves his purſuers ſo far behind, that he
might probably have eſcaped; but taking into
a thick wood, his horns were entangled in the
branches, where he was held till the hounds
came up, and tore him in pieces. In his laſt mo-
ments, he thus exclaimed—How ill do we judge
of our own true advantages! the *legs* which I *de-
ſpiſed* would have borne me away in ſafety, had
not my *favourite antlers* betrayed me to ruin.

FABLE XIV.

The Swallow and other Birds.

A Swallow obſerving an huſbandman employed in ſowing hemp, called the little Birds
together, and informed them what the farmer
was about. He told them that hemp was the
material from which the nets, ſo fatal to the fea-
thered race, were compoſed; and adviſed them
unanimouſly to join in picking it up, in order
to prevent the conſequences. The Birds either
diſbelieving his information, or neglecting his
advice, gave themſelves no trouble about the
matter. In a little time the hemp appeared above
ground: the friendly Swallow again addreſſed

C

himſelf

himfelf to them, told them it was not yet too late, provided they would immediately fet about the work, before the feeds had taken too deep root. But they ftill rejecting his advice, he forfook their fociety, repaired for fafety to towns and cities, *there* built his habitation and kept his refidence. One day, as he was fkimming along the ftreets, he happened to fee a large parcel of thofe very Birds, imprifoned in a cage, on the fhoulders of a bird-catcher. Unhappy wretches, faid he, you *now feel* the punifhment of your former neglect. But thofe, who, having no forefight of their own, defpife the wholefome admonition of their friends, deferve the mifchief which their own obftinacy or negligence brings upon their heads.

F A B L E XV.

The Afs and the Lap-dog.

AN Afs, who lived in the fame houfe with a favourite Lap-dog, obferving the fuperior degree of affection which the little minion enjoyed, imagined he had nothing more to do, in order to obtain an equal fhare, in the good graces of the family, than to imitate the Lap-dog's playful and endearing careffes. Accordingly, he began to frifk about before his mafter, kicking up

his

13 The Stag drinking.
14 The Swallow & other Birds.
15 The Ass and the Lap Dog.
16 The Lion and the Mouse.
17 The Wolf and the Crane.
18 Countryman and Snake.
19 The Dog & the Shadow.
20 The Sun & the Wind.
21 The Wolf & the Mastiff.
22 Fortune & the Schoolboy
23 The Frog and the Ox.
24 Lion & other Beasts hunting.

his heels and braying, in an aukward affectation
of wantonnefs and pleafantry. This ftrange behaviour could not fail of raifing much laughter,
which the Afs miftaking for approbation and encouragement, he procceded to leap upon his
mafter's breaft, and began very familiarly to lick
his face: but he was prefently convinced by the
force of a good cudgel, that what is fprightly
and agreeable in *one*, may in *another* be juftly
cenfured as rude and impertinent; and that the
fureft way to gain efteem, is for every one to act
fuitably to his own natural genius and character.

F A B L E XVI.

The Lion and the Moufe.

A Lion by accident laid his paw upon a poor
innocent Moufe. The frighted little creature, imagining fhe was juft going to be devoured, begged hard for her life, urged that
clemency was the faireft attribute of power, and
earneftly intreated his majefty not to ftain his illuftrious paws with the blood of fo infignificant
an animal: upon which, the Lion very generoufly fet her at liberty. It happened a few days
afterwards, that the Lion ranging for his prey,
fell into the toils of the hunter. The Moufe
heard his roarings, knew the voice of her bene-
C 2
factor,

factor, and immediately repairing to his affiftance gnawed in pieces the mefhes of the net, and by delivering her preferver, convinced him that there is no creature fo much below another, but may have it in his power to return a good office.

FABLE XVII.

The Wolf and the Crane.

A Wolf having with too much greedinefs fwallowed a bone, it unfortunately ftuck in his throat; and in the violence of his pain he applied to feveral animals, earneftly intreating them to extract it. None cared to hazard the dangerous experiment, except the Crane; who, perfuaded by his folemn promifes of a gratuity, ventured to thruft her enormous length of neck down his throat, and having fuccefsfully performed the operation, claimed the recompence. See the unreafonablenefs of fome creatures, faid the Wolf: have I not fuffered thee fafely to draw thy *neck* out of my *jaws,* and haft thou the confcience to demand a *further* reward!

FABLE XVIII.

The Countryman and the Snake.

AN honeſt Countryman oberved a Snake ly-ing under a hedge, almoſt frozen to death. He was moved with compaſſion; and bringing it home, he laid it near the fire, and gave it ſome new milk. Thus fed and cheriſhed, the creature preſently began to revive: but no ſooner had he recovered ſtrength enough to do miſchief, than he ſprung upon the Contryman's wife, bit one of his children, and in ſhort, threw all the whole family into confuſion and terror. Un-greatful wretch! ſaid the man, thou haſt ſuffi-ciently taught me how *ill-judged* it is, to confer benefits on the *worthleſs* and *undeſerving*. So ſay-ing, he ſnatched up a hatchet, and cut the Snake in pieces.

FABLE XIX.

The Dog and the Shadow.

AN hungry Spaniel, having ſtolen a piece of fleſh from a butchers's ſhop, was carrying it acroſs a river. The water being clear, and the ſun ſhining brightly, he ſaw his own Image in the ſtream, and fancied it to be another dog,

C 3

with

with a more delicious morfel: upon which, *un-juftly* and *greedily* opening his jaws to fnatch at the *fhadow*, he loft the *fubftance*.

F A B L E XX.

The Sun and the Wind.

PHOEBUS and AEolus had once a difpute, which of them could fooneft prevail with a certain traveller to part with his cloak. AEolus began the attack, and affaulted him with great violence. But the man wrapping his cloak ftill clofer about him, doubled his efforts to keep it, and went on his way. And now Phœbus darted his warm infinuating rays, which melting the traveller by degrees, at length obliged him to throw afide that cloak, which all the rage of AEolus could not compel him to refign. Learn hence, faid Phœbus to the bluftering god, that *foft* and *gentle means* will often accomplifh, what *force* and *fury* can never effect.

F A B L E XXI.

The Wolf and the Maftiff.

A Lean half-ftarved wolf inadvertently ftrolled in the way of a ftrong well-fed Maftiff. The Wolf being much too weak to act upon the
offenfive.

offensive, thought it most prudent to accost honest Towser in a friendly manner: and among
other civilities, very complaisantly congratulated
him on his goodly appearance. Why, yes, returned the Mastiff, I am indeed in tolerable case;
and if you will follow me, you may soon be altogether in as good a plight. The Wolf pricked
up his ears at the proposal, and requested to be
informed what he must do to earn such plentiful
meals. Very little, replied the Mastiff; only
drive away beggars, caress my master, and be
civil to his family. To these conditions the hungry Wolf had no objection, and very readily
consented to follow his new acquaintance whereever he would conduct him. As they were trotting along, the Wolf observed that the hair was
worn in a circle round his friend's neck; which
raised his curiosity to enquire what was the occasion of it. Nothing, answered the Mastiff, or
a mere trifle; perhaps the collar to which my
chain is sometimes fastened. *Chain!* replied the
Wolf, with much surprize; it should seem then
that you are not permitted to rove about where
and when you please. Not always, returned
Towser, hanging down his head; but what does
that signify? it signifies so much, rejoined the
Wolf, that I am resolved to have no share in

C 4

your

your dinners; *half* a meal with *liberty*, is in my eftimation, preferable to a *full* one *without* it.

F A B L E XXII.

Fortune and the School-boy.

A School-boy, fatigued with play, threw himfelf down by the brink of a deep pit, where
he fell faft afleep. Fortune happening to pafs
by, faw him in this dangerous fituation, and
kindly gave him a tap on the fhoulder: My dear
child, faid fhe, if you had fallen into this pit, I
fhould have borne the blame; though in fact, the
accident would have been wholly owing to your
own careleffnefs.

Misfortune, faid a celebrated cardinal, is but
another word for imprudence. The maxim is by
no means abfolutely true: certain however, it
is, that mankind fuffer more evils from their own
imprudence, than from events which it is not in
their power to controul.

F A B L E XXIII.

The Frog and the Ox.

A Frog being wonderfully ftruck with the fize
and majefty of an Ox, that was grazing in
the marfhes, could not forbear endeavouring to

expand

expand herself to the same portly magnitude. After puffing and swelling for some time: " What think you, sister," said she, "will this do?" Far from it. "Will this?" By no means. "But this surely will." Nothing like it. In short, after many ridiculous efforts to the same fruitlefs purpose, the simple Frog burst her *skin*, and miserably expired upon the spot.

F A B L E XXIV.

The Lion and other Beasts hunting in partnership.

A Leopard, a Lynx, and a Wolf were ambitious of the honour of hunting with the Lion. His savage majesty graciously condescended to their desire, and it was agreed that they should all have an equal share in whatever might be taken. They scour the forest, are unanimous in the pursuit; and, after a very fine chase, pulled down a noble stag. It was divided with great dexterity by the Lynx, into four equal parts; but just as each was going to secure his share— Hold, says the Lion, let no one presume to serve himself, till he hath heard our *just* and *reasonable* claims. I seize upon the first quarter by virtue of my *prerogative;* the second I think is due to my superior *conduct* and *courage;* I cannot forego the third on account of the *necessities* of my den;

and

and if any one is inclined to difpute my right to the fourth, let him fpeak. Awed by the majefty of his frown, and the terror of his paws, they filently withdrew, refolving never to hunt again but with their *equals.*

FABLE XXV.

The Ant and the Fly.

AN Ant and a Fly had once a ridiculous conteft about precedency, and were arguing which of the two was the more honourable: fuch difputes moft frequently happen amongft the loweft and moft worthlefs creatures. The Fly expreffed great refentment, that fuch a poor crawling infect fhould prefume to lie bafking in the fame funfhine, with one fo much her fuperior! Thou haft not furely the infolence, faid fhe, to imagine thyfelf of an equal rank with *me.* I am none of your mechanic creatures who live by their induftry; but enjoy in plenty, and without labour, every thing that is truely delicious. I place myfelf uncontrouled upon the hands of kings; I kifs with freedom the lips of beauties; and feaft upon the choiceft facrifices that are offered to the gods. To eat with the gods, replyed the Ant, and to enjoy the favours of the fair and the powerful, would be great honour

indeed

indeed to one who was an invited, or a welcome gueſt; but an impertinent intruder, who is driven out with averſion and contempt where-ever he appears, has not much cauſe methinks to boaſt of his privileges. And as to the honour of not labouring for your ſubſiſtence; here too your *boaſt* is only your *diſgrace*; for hence it is, that one half of the year you are deſtitute even of the common neceſſaries of life; whilſt I, at the ſame time, returning to the hoarded granaries which my *honeſt induſtry* has filled, enjoy every ſatisfaction, independent of the favour, either of *beauties* or of *kings*.

F A B L E XXVI.

The Bear and the two Friends.

TWO Friends, ſetting out together upon a journey which led through a dangerous *foreſt*, mutually promiſed to aſſiſt each other, if they ſhould happen to be aſſaulted. They had not proceeded far, before they perceived a Bear making towards them with great rage. There were no hopes in flight; but one of them, being very active, ſprung up into a tree; upon which, the other, throwing himſelf flat on the ground, held his breath, and pretended to be dead; remembering to have heard it *aſſerted*, that this crea-

true

ture will not prey upon a *dead* carcafe. The Bear came up, and after fmelling to him fome time, left him, and went on. When he was fairly out of fight and hearing, the hero from the tree calls out—Well, my Friend, what faid the Bear? He feemed to whifper you very clofely. He did fo, replied the other, and gave me this good piece of advice; never to affociate with a *wretch,* who in the hour of *danger* will defert his Friend.

F A B L E XXVII.

The Bull and the Gnat.

A Conceited Gnat, fully perfuaded of his own importance, having placed himfelf on the horn of a Bull, expreffed great uneafinefs left his weight fhould be incommodious; and with much ceremony begged the Bull'spardon for the liberty he had taken; affuring him that he would immediately remove, if he preffed too hard upon him. Give yourfelf no uneafinefs on that account, replied the Bull, I befeech you: for as I never perceived when you *fate down,* I fhall probably not mifs you whenever you think fit to *rife up.*

FABLE

25. Ant and the Fly.
26. Travellers & the Bear.
27. Bull and the Gnat.
28. Bees and Wasps.
29. Old Man and Death.
30. Court and Country Mouse.
31. Goat and Fox.
32. The Stork and Cranes.
33. Oak and Willow.
34. The Boy and Filberts.
35. Satyr and Traveller.
36. Mouse and Stag.

FABLE XXVIII.

The Wasps and the Bees.

PRETENDERS of every kind are beſt detected by appealing to their works.

Some honey-combs being claimed by a ſwarm of Waſps, the right owners proteſted againſt their demand, and the cauſe was referred to a Hornet. Witneſſes being examined, they depoſed that certain winged creatures, who had a loud hum, were of a yellowiſh colour, and ſomewhat like Bees, were obſerved a conſiderable time hovering about the place where this neſt was found. But this did not ſufficiently deſide the queſtion; for theſe characteriſtics, the Hornet obſerved, agreed no leſs with the Bees than with the Waſps. At length a ſenſible old Bee offered to put the matter upon this deciſive iſſue; Let a place be appointed, by the court, ſaid he, for the plaintiffs and defendants to work in: it will then ſoon appear which of us are capable of forming ſuch regular cells, and afterwards of filling them with ſo delicious a fluid. The Waſps refuſing to agree to this propoſal, ſufficiently convinced the judge on which ſide the right lay: and he decreed the honey-combs accordingly.

FABLE.

FABLE XXIX.

The Old Man and Death.

A Feeble Old Man, quite spent with carrying a burthen of sticks, which with much labour he had gathered in a neighbouring wood, called upon Death to release him from the fatigues he endured. Death hearing the invocation, was immediately at his elbow, and asked him what he wanted. Frighted and trembling at the unexpected appearance—O good sir! said he, my burthen had like to have slipt from me, and being unable to recover it myself, I only implored your assistance to *replace it on my shoulders.*

FABLE XXX.

The Court and Country-Mouse.

A Contented Country-Mouse had once the honour to receive a visit from an old acquaintance belonging to the Court. The Country-Mouse, extremely glad to see her guest, very hospitably set before her the best cheese and bacon which her cottage afforded; and as to their beverage, it was the purest water from the spring. The repast was *homely* indeed, but the welcome *hearty:* they sate and chatted away the evening

together

together very agreeably, and then retired in *peace and quietness* each to her little cell. The next morning when the guest was to take her leave, she kindly pressed her country friend to accompany her; setting forth in very pompous terms, the great *elegance* and *plenty* in which she lived at Court. The Country-Mouse was easily prevailed upon, and they set out together. It was late in the evening when they arrived at the palace; however, in one of the rooms, they found the remains of a sumptuous entertainment. There were creams, and jellies, and sweetmeats; and every thing, in short, of the most delicate kind: the cheese was Parmesan: and they wetted their whiskers in exquisite Champaign. But before they had half finished their repast, they were alarmed with the barking and scratching of a lapdog; then the mewing of a cat frightened them almost to death; by and by, a whole train of servants burst into the room: and every thing was swept away in an instant. Ah! my dear friend, said the Country-Mouse, as soon as she had recovered courage enough to speak, if your *fine living* is thus interrupted with *fears* and *dangers*, let me return to my plain food, and my peaceful cottage; for what is *elegance* without *ease*; or *plenty*, with an *aching heart*.

FABLE

FABLE XXXI.

The Fox and the Goat.

A Fox and a Goat travelling together, in a very
sultry day, found themselves exceedingly
thirsty; when looking round the country in order to discover a place where they might probably
meet with water, they at length descried a clear
spring at the bottom of a pit. They both eagerly
descended, and having sufficiently allayed their
thirst, began to consider how they should get
out. Many expedients for that purpose were
mutually proposed, and rejected. At last the
crafty Fox cried out with great joy, I have a
thought just struck into my mind, which I am
confident will extricate us out of our difficulty:
do you, said he to the Goat, only rear yourself up
upon your hinder legs, and rest your fore feet
against the side of the pit. In this posture, I will
climb up to your head, from whence, I shall be
able, with a spring, to reach the top: and when
I am once there. you are sensible it will be very
easy for me to pull you out by the horns. The
simple Goat liked the proposal well; and immediately placed himself as directed: by means of
which, the Fox without much difficulty, gained
the top. And now, said the Goat, give me the

assistance

affiftance you promifed. Thou old fool, replied the Fox, hadft thou but half as much brains as beard, thou wouldft never have believed that I would hazard my *own life* to fave *thine*. However, I will leave with thee a piece of advice, which may be of fervice to thee hereafter, if thou fhouldft have the good fortune to make thy efcape; "Never venture into a pit again, before thou haft well confidered how to get out of it."

F A B L E   XXXII.

The Farmer, the Cranes, and the Stork.

A Stork was unfortunately drawn into company with fome Cranes, who were juft fetting out on a party of pleafure, as they called it, which in truth was to rob the fifh-ponds of a neighbouring Farmer. Our fimple Stork agreed to make one; and it fo happened, that they were all taken in the fact. The Cranes having been old offenders, had very little to fay for themfelves, and were prefently difpatched: but the Stork pleaded hard for his life. He urged that it was his firft fault, that he was not naturally addicted to ftealing fifh, that he was famous for piety to his parents, and in fhort, for many other virtues. Your *piety* and *virtue*, faid the Farmer, may for aught I know be exemplary; but your being

D

in company with thieves renders it very fufpicious; and you muft therefore fubmit with patience to fhare the *fame punifhment* with your *companions.*

FABLE XXXIII.

The Oak and the Willow.

A Conceited Willow had once the vanity to challenge his mighty neighbour the Oak, to a trial of ftrength. It was to be determined by the next ftorm; and AEolus was addreffed by both parties, to exert his moft powerful efforts. This was no fooner afked than granted; and a violent hurricane arofe: when the pliant Willow, bending from the blaft, or fhrinking under it, evaded all its force: while the generous Oak, difdaining to give way, oppofed its fury, and was torn up by the roots. Immediately the Willow began to exult and to claim the victory: when thus the fallen Oak interrupted his exultation. Calleft thou this a trial of *ftrength?* Poor wretch! not to thy *ftrength*, but *weaknefs;* not to thy boldly facing danger, but meanly fkulking from it, thou oweft thy *prefent fafety.* I am an Oak, though fallen; thou ftill a Willow, though unhurt: but who, except fo mean a wretch as thyfelf, would prefer an *ignominious life*, preferved by craft or cowardice, to the *glory* of meeting *death* in an *honourable caufe.*   FABLE

FABLE XXXIV.

The Boy and the Filberts.

A Certain Boy, as Epictetus tells the fable, put his hand into a pitcher, where great plenty of Figs and Filberts were depofited: he grafped as many as his fift could poffible hold, but when he endeavoured to pull it out, the narrownefs of the neck prevented him. Unwilling to lofe any of them, but unable to draw out his hand, he burft into tears, and bitterly bemoaned his hard fortune. An honeft fellow who ftood by, gave him this wife and reafonable advice;—Grafp only *half* the quantity, my Boy, and you will *eafily fucceed.*

FABLE XXXV.

The Satyr and the Traveller.

A Poor Man travelling in the depth of winter, through a dreary foreft, no inn to receive him, no human creature to befriend or comfort him, was in danger of being ftarved to death. At laft however he came to the cave of a Satyr, where he intreated leave to reft a while, and fhelter himfelf from the inclemency of the weather. The Satyr very civilly complied with his

D 2   requeft.

requeſt. The Man had no ſooner entered, than he began to blow his fingers. His hoſt, ſurprized at the novelty of the action, was curious to know the meaning of it. I do it, ſaid the Traveller, to *warm* my frozen joints, which are benumbed with cold. Preſently afterwards the Satyr having perpared a meſs of *hot gruel* to refreſh his gueſt, the Man found it neceſſary to blow his porridge too. What, inquired the Satyr, is not your gruel *hot* enough? Yes, replied the Traveller, too hot; and I blow it to make it *cooler.* Do you ſo? quoth the Satyr, then get out of my cave as faſt as you can; for I deſire to have no communication with a creature that blows *hot* and *cold* with the *ſame breath.*

F A B L E XXXVI.

The Horſe and the Stag.

BEFORE the uſe of Horſes was known in the world, one of theſe noble animals. having been inſulted by a Stag, and finding himſelf unequal to his adverſary, applied to a man for aſſiſtance. The requeſt was eaſily granted, and the man putting a bridle in his mouth, and mounting upon his back, ſoon came up with the Stag, and laid him dead at his enemy's feet. The Horſe having thus gratified his revenge, thanked

his

his auxiliary: And now will I return in triumph, said he, and reign the undisputed lord of the forest. By no means, replied the man; I shall have occasion for your services, and you must go home with me. So saying, he led him to his hovel, where the unhappy Steed spent the remainder of his days in a *laborious servitude;* sensible too late, " That how pleasing soever revenge may appear, it always costs more to a generous mind than the purchase is worth."

FABLE XXXVII.

The Farmer and his Sons.

A Wealthy old Farmer, who had for some time declined in his health, perceiving that he had not many days to live, called his Sons together to his bed side. My dear Children, said the dying Man, I leave it with you as my last injunction, not to part with the farm which has been in our family these hundred years: for, to disclose to you a secret which I received from my father, and which I now think proper to communicate to you, there is a treasure hid somewhere in the grounds; though I never could discover the particular spot where it lies concealed. However, as soon as the harvest is got in, spare no pains in the search, and I am well

assured

affured you will not lofe your labour. The wife old Man was no fooner laid in his grave, and the time he mentioned arrived, than his Sons went to work, and with great vigour and alacrity, turned up again and again every foot of ground belonging to their farm: the confequence of which was, although they did not find the object of their purfuit, that their lands yielded a far more *plentiful crop* than thofe of their neighbours. At the end of the year, when they were fettling their accounts, and computing their extraordinary profits, I would venture a wager, faid one of the brothers more acute than the reft, that this was the *concealed wealth* my father meant. I am fure, at leaft, we have found by experience, that " *Induftry is itfelf a treafure.*"

FABLE XXXVIII.

The Lion and Gnat.

AVAUNT! thou paltry, contemptible infect! faid a proud Lion one day to a Gnat that was frifking about in the air near his den. The Gnat, enraged at this unprovoked infult, vowed revenge, and immediately darted into the Lion's ear. After having fufficiently teized him in that quarter, fhe quitted her ftation and retired under his belly; and from thence made

her

her laſt and moſt formidable attack in his noſ-
trils, where ſtinging him almoſt to madneſs, the
Lion at length fell down, utterly ſpent with
rage, vexation, and pain. The Gnat having thus
abundantly gratified her reſentment, flew off in
great exultation: but in the heedleſs tranſports
of her ſucceſs, not ſufficiently attending to her
own ſecurity, ſhe found herſelf unexpectedly
entangled in the web of a ſpider; who ruſhing
out inſtantly upon her, put an end to her *triumph*
and her *life*.

This fable inſtructs us, never to ſuffer ſucceſs
ſo far to tranſport us, as to throw us off our
guard againſt a reverſe of fortune.

F A B L E XXXIX.

The Miſer and his Treaſure.

A Miſer having ſcraped together a conſiderable
ſum of money, by denying himſelf the common conveniencies of life, was much embarraſſed
where to lodge it moſt ſecurely. After many
perplexing debates with himſelf, he at length
fixed upon a corner in a retired field, where he
depoſited his *Treaſure*, and with it his *heart*, in a
hole which he dug for that purpoſe. His mind
was now for a moment at eaſe; but he had not

D 4

proceeded

proceeded many paces in his way home, when all his anxiety returned; and he could not forbear going back to fee that every thing was fafe. This he repeated again and again; till he was at laft obferved by a labourer who was mending a hedge in an adjacent meadow. The fellow concluding that fomething extraordinary muft be the occafion of thefe frequent vifits, marked the fpot; and coming in the night in order to examine it, he difcovered the prize, and bore it off unmolefted. Early the next morning, the Mifer again renewed his vifit; when finding his Treafure gone, he broke out into the moft bitter exclamations. A traveller, who happened to be paffing by at the fame time, was moved by his complaints to enquire into the caufe of them. Alas! replied the Mifer. I have fuftained the moft cruel and irreparable lofs! fome villain has robbed me of a fum of money, which I *buried* under this ftone no longer ago than yefterday. *Buried!* returned the traveller with furprize; a very extraordinary method truly of difpofing of your riches! Why did you not rather keep them in your houfe, that they might be ready for your daily occafions? *Daily occafions!* refumed the Mifer, with an air of much indignation; do you imagine I fo little know the value of money, as to fuffer it to be run away with by *occafions?* on the

contrary,

contrary, I had *prudently* refolved not touch a
fingle fhilling of it. If that was your *wife* refolution, anfwered the traveller, I fee no fort of
reafon for your being thus afflicted: it is but putting *this ftone* in the place of your Treafure, and
it will anfwer all your purpofes full as well.

FABLE XI.

Minerva's Olive.

THE gods, fay the heathen mythologifts,
have each of them their favourite tree. Jupiter preferred the Oak, Venus the Myrtle, and
Phœbus the Laurel; Cybele the Pine, and Hercules the Poplar. Minerva, continues the mythologifts, furprized they fhould choofe *barren
trees*, afked Jupiter the reafon.—It is, faid he,
to prevent any fufpicion that we confer the
honour we do them, from an interefted motive.
Let folly fufpect what it pleafes, returned Minerva;
I fhall not fcruple to acknowledge that I make
choice of the Olive for the *ufefulnefs of its fruit.*
O daughter, replied the father of the gods, it is
with juftice that men efteem thee wife; for nothing is truly *valuable* that is not *ufeful.*

FABLE

FABLE XLI.

The Mimick and the Countryman.

MEN often judge wrong from some foolish prejudice; and whilst they persist in the defence of their mistakes, are sometimes brought to shame by incontestible evidence.

A certain wealthy patrician, intending to treat the Roman people with some theatrical entertainments, published a reward to any one who could furnish a new or uncommon diversion. Excited by emulation, the artists assembled from all parts; among whom, a Mimick, well known for his arch wit, gave out that he had a kind of entertainment that had never yet been produced upon any stage.

This report being spread about, brought the whole city together. The theatre could hardly contain the number of spectators. And when the artist appeared alone upon the stage, without any apparatus, without any prompter or assistant, curiosity and suspence kept the spectators in a profound silence.

On

37. Sick-man and Sons.

38. Lion & Gnat.

39. Miser & his Treasure.

40. Minerva and the Olive.

41. The Mimicks.

42. Dog & Crocodile.

43. Wolf in disguise.

44. Bee and Spider.

45. Ass and his Master.

46. Cock and Fox.

47. The Eagle and Crow.

48. The Farmer and Stag.

On a fudden the performer thruft down his
head into his bofom, and mimicked the fqueak-
ing of a young pig fo naturally, that the audience infifted upon it, he had one under his cloak,
and ordered him to be fearched.   Which being
done, and nothing appearing, they loaded the
man with encomiums, and honoured him with
the moft extravagant applaufe.

A Country fellow obferving what paffed——
"Faith, fays he, I can do this better than he:"
and immediately gave out that he would perform
the fame much better the next day.   Accordingly, greater crowds affembled: prepoffeffed
however in favour of the firft artift, they fit prepared to laugh at the Clown, rather than to
judge fairly of his performance.

They both came out upon the ftage.   The
Mimick grunts away firft, is received with vaft
applaufe, and the loudeft acclamations. Then the
Countryman pretending that he concealed a little pig under his cloak, (which in fact he did)
pinched the ear of the animal, till he made him
fqueak.   The people exclaimed aloud that the
firft performer had imitated the pig much more
naturally, and would have hiffed the Countryman off the ftage: but he produced the real pig

from

from his bofom, and convinced them by a vifible proof of their ridiculous error; *See, Gentlemen,* faid he, *What pretty fort of judges you are!*

FABLE XLII.

The Dog and the Crocodile.

WE can never be too carefully guarded againft a connection with perfons of an ill character.

As a Dog was courfing the banks of the Nile, he grew thirfty; but, fearing to be feized by the monfters of that river, he would not ftop to fatiate his drought, but lapped as he ran. A Crocodile, raifing his head above the furface of the water, afked him, Why he was in fuch a hurry? He had often, he faid, wifhed for his acquaintance, and fhould be glad to embrace the prefent opportunity. You do me great honour, faid the Dog, but it is to *avoid* fuch companions as you, that I am in fo much hafte.

FABLE XLIII.

The Wolf in Difguife.

DESIGNING hypocrites frequently lay themfelves open to difcovery, by over-acting their parts.

A Wolf who by his frequent vifits to a flock of fheep in his neighbourhood, began to be extremely well known to them, thought it expedient, for the more fuccefsfully carrying on his depredations, to appear in a new character. To this end he difguifed himfelf in a fhepherd's habit; and refting his fore-feet upon a ftick, which ferved him by way of crook, he foftly made his approaches towards the fold. It happened that the fhepherd and his dog were both of them extended on the grafs, faft afleep; fo that he would certainly have fucceeded in his project, if he had not imprudently attempted to imitate the fhepherd's voice. The horrid noife awakened them both: when the Wolf, encumbered with his difguife, and finding it impoffible either to refift or to flee, yielded up his life an eafy prey to the fhepherd's dog.

FABLE

FABLE XLIV.

The Bee and the Spider.

THE Bee and the Spider once entered into a warm debate, which was the better artift. The Spider urged her fkill in the mathematics; and afferted that no one was half fo well acquainted as herfelf with the conftruction of lines, angles, fquares, and circles: that the web fhe daily wove was a fpecimen of art inimitable by any other creature in the univerfe: and befides, that her works were derived from herfelf alone, the product of her own bowels; whereas the boafted honey of the Bee was ftolen from every herb and flower of the field; nay. that fhe had obligations even to the meaneft weeds. To this the Bee replied, that fhe was in hopes the art of extracting honey from the meaneft weeds would at leaft have been allowed her as an excellence; and that as to her ftealing fweets from the herbs and flowers of the field, her fkill was there fo confpicuous, that no flower ever fuffered the leaft diminution of its fragrance from fo delicate an operation. Then, as to the Spider's vaunted knowledge in the conftruction of lines and angles, fhe believed fhe might fafely reft the merits of her caufe, on the regularity alone of her combs; but fince fhe could

add

add to this, the fweetnefs and excellence of her honey, and the various purpofes to which her wax was employed, fhe had nothing to fear from a comparifon of her fkill with that of the weaver of a flimfy cobweb; for the *value* of every art, fhe obferved, is chiefly to be eftimated by its *ufe*.

F A B L E   XLV.

The Afs and his Mafter.

A Diligent Afs, daily loaded beyond his ftrength by a fevere Mafter, whom he had long ferved, and who kept him at very fhort commons, happened one day in his old age to be oppreffed with a more than ordinary burthen of earthen-ware. His ftrength being much impaired, and the road deep and uneven, he unfortunately made a trip, and unable to recover himfelf, fell down, and broke all the veffels to pieces. His Mafter tranfported with rage, began to beat him moft unmercifully Againft whom the poor Afs, lifting up his head as he lay on the ground, thus ftrongly remonftrated: Unfeeling wretch! to thy own *avaricious cruelty*, in firft pinching me of food, and then loading me beyond my ftrength, thou oweft the *misfortune* which thou fo unjuftly imputeft to me.

FABLE XLVI.

The Cock and the Fox.

AN experienced old Cock was settling himself to roost upon a high bough, when a Fox appeared under the tree. I am come, said the artful hypocrite, to acquaint you in the name of all my brethren, that a general peace is concluded between your whole family and ours. Descend immediately I beseech you, that we may mutually embrace upon so joyful and unexpected an event. My good friend, replied the Cock, nothing could be more agreeable to me than this news: and to hear it from you increases my satisfaction. But I perceive two hounds at a distance coming this way, who are probably dispatched as couriers with the treaty: as they run very swiftly, and will certainly be here in a few minutes, I will wait their arrival, that we may all four embrace together. Reynard well knew, if that was the case, it was no time for him to remain there any longer: pretending therefore to be in great haste; Adieu, said he, for the present; we will refer our rejoicing to *another opportunity:* upon which he darted into the woods with all imaginable expedition. Old Chanticleer no sooner saw him depart, than he crowed abundantly

in the triumph of his artifice: for by a harmlefs
ftratagem to *difappoint* the malevolent intentions
of thofe who are endeavouring to deceive us to
our ruin, is not only *innocent*, but *laudable*.

FABLE XLVII.

The Eagle and the Crow.

TO miftake our own talents, or over-rate our
abilities, is always *ridiculous*, and fometimes
dangerous.

An Eagle, from the top of a high mountain,
made a ftoop at a lamb, pounced it, and bore
it away to her young. A Crow, who had built
her neft in a cedar near the foot of the rock, obferving what paffed, was ambitious of performing the fame exploit: and darting from her neft,
fixed her talons in the fleece of another lamb.
But neither able to move her prey, nor difen-
tangle her feet, fhe was taken by the fhepherd,
and carried away for his children to play with:
who eagerly enquiring what bird it was,—An
hour ago, faid he, fhe fancied herfelf an *Eagle*;
however, I fuppofe fhe is by this time convinced
that fhe is but a *Crow*.

E   FABLE

FABLE XLVIII.

The Farmer and the Stag.

A Stag, who had left at some distance a pack of hounds, came up to a Farmer, and desired he would suffer him to hide himself in a little coppice which joined to his house. The Farmer, on condition that he would forbear to enter a field of wheat, which lay before him, and was now ready for the sickle, immediately gave him leave, and promised not to betray him. The squire with his train instantly appeared, and enquired whether he had not seen the Stag; No, said the Farmer, he has not passed this way, I assure you: but, in order to curry favour at the same time with his worship, he *pointed slily* with his finger to the place where the poor beast lay concealed. This however, the sportsman, intent on his game, did not observe, but passed on with his dogs across the very field. As soon as the Stag perceived they were gone, he prepared to steal off, without speaking a word. Methinks, cryed the Farmer, you might *thank me*, at least, for the refuge I have afforded you: yes, said the Stag, and had your *hands* been as honest as your *tongue*, I certainly should; but all the return that

a *double dealer* has to expect, is a juft *indignation*
and *contempt.*

F A B L E XLIX.

The Lion, the Tyger, and the Fox.

A Lion and a Tyger jointly feized on a young
fawn, which they immediately killed. This
they had no fooner performed, than they fell a
fighting, in order to decide whofe property it
fhould be. The battle was fo bloody, and fo
obftinate, that they were both compelled, thro'
wearinefs and lofs of blood, to defift; and lye
down by mutual confent, *totally difabled.* At this
inftant, a Fox unluckily came by; who, perceiving their fituation, made bold to feize the
contefted prey, and bore it off unmolefted. As
foon as the Lion could recover breath—How
foolifh, faid he, has been our conduct! Inftead
of being contented as we ought, with our *refpec-*
tive fhares; our fenfelefs rage has rendered us unable to prevent this rafcally Fox from defrauding
us of *the whole.*

FABLE L.

The Lion and the Ass.

A Conceited Ass had once the impertinence
to bray forth some contemptuous speeches
against the Lion. The suddenness of the insult,
at first raised some emotions of wrath in his breast;
but turning his head and perceiving from whence
it came, they immediately subsided; and he very
sedately walked on, without deigning to honour
the contemptible creature, even so much as with
an *angry word.*

FABLE LI.

The Snake and the Hedge-hog.

IT is by no means prudent to join interests
with such as have it in their power to impose
upon us their own conditions.

By the intreaties of a Hedge-hog half starved
with cold, a Snake was once persuaded to receive him into her cell. He was no sooner entered, than his prickles began to be very uneasy
to his companion: upon which, the Snake desired he would provide himself another lodging,
as she found her apartment was not large enough

to accommodate both. Nay, faid the Hedge-hog, let them that are *uneafy* in their fituation exchange it; for my own part, I am very well *contented* where I am; and if you are not, you are welcome to remove whenever you think proper.

FABLE LII.

The Trumpeter.

A Trumpeter in a certain army, happened to be taken prifoner. He was ordered immediately to execution, but pleaded in excufe for himfelf, that it was unjuft a perfon fhould fuffer death, who, far from an intention of mifchief, did not even wear an offenfive weapon. So much the rather, replied one of the enemy, fhalt thou die; fince without any defign of *fighting thyfelf*, thou exciteft others to the *bloody bufinefs:* for he that is the *abettor* of a bad action, is at leaft equally guilty with him that *commits* it.

FABLE

FABLE LIII.

** Vice and Fortune.*

FORTUNE and Vice, according to Plutarch had once a violent conteſt, which of them had it moſt in their power to make mankind unhappy. Fortune boaſted that ſhe could take from men every external good; and bring upon them every external evil. Be it ſo, replied Vice; but this is by no means ſufficient to make them miſerable without my aſſiſtance : whereas without yours, I am able to render them completely ſo; nay, in ſpite too of all your endeavours to make them happy.

FABLE LIV.

The Bear and the Bees.

A Bear happened to be ſtung by a Bee; the pain was ſo acute, that in the madneſs of revenge he ran into the garden, and overturned the hive, vowing the deſtruction of the whole race. This outrage provoked their anger to a high degree, and brought the fury of the whole

* *This fable is abridged from Plutarch, by Lord Bolingbroke, in his Philoſophical Tracts.*

ſwarm

swarm upon him.   They attacked him with such violence, that his life was in danger, and it was with the utmoſt difficulty that he made his eſcape, wounded from head to tail.   In this deſperate condition, lamenting his misfortune, and licking his ſores, he could not forbear reflecting, how much more adviſeable it had been to have patiently acquieſced under *one* injury, than thus by an unprofitable reſentment to have provoked a *thouſand*.

E 4

49 Lion Tyger
& Fox.

50. Ass and
Lion.

51 Snake &
Hedgehog.

52 Trumpeter
taken prisoner.

53 Doe and
Fortune.

54 Boar and
Bees.

FABLES.

BOOK II.

FROM THE

MODERNS.

FABLE I.

The Miller, his Son, and their Ass.

A Miller and his Son were driving their Ass to market, in order to sell him: and that he might get thither fresh and in good condition, they drove him on gently before them. They had not gone far, when they met a company of travellers. Sure, say they, you are mighty careful of your Ass: methinks one of you might as well get up and ride, as suffer him to walk on at his ease, while you trudge after him on foot. In compliance with this advice, the Old Man set his Son upon the beast. They had scarce advanced a quarter of a mile further, when

they

they met another company. You idle young
rogue, faid one of the party, why don't you
get down, and let your poor father ride? Upon
this, the Old Man made his Son difmount, and
got up himfelf. While they were marching in
this manner, a third company began to infult
the father. You hard-hearted, unnatural wretch,
fay they, how can you fuffer that poor lad to
wade through the dirt, while you like an alder-
man ride at your eafe? The good-natured Miller ftood corrected, and immediately took his
Son up behind him. And now, the next man
they met exclaimed with more vehemence, than
all the reft. Was there ever fuch a couple of
lazy boobies? to overload in fo unconfcionable
a manner, a poor dumb creature, who is far lefs
able to carry them than they are to carry him!
The complying Old Man would have been
half inclined to make the trial, had not experience by this time fufficiently convinced him,
that there cannot be a more *fruitlefs* attempt,
than to endeavour to pleafe all man'.ind.

FABLE

FABLE II.

The Sorceress.

NIGHT and silence had now given repose to the whole world; when an old illnatured Sorceress, in order to exercise her infernal arts, entered into a gloomy wood, that trembled at her approach. The scene of her horrid incantations was within the circumference of a large circle; in the center of which an altar was raised, where the hallowed vervain blazed in trianglar flames, while the mischievous *Hag* pronounced the dreadful words, which bound all hell in obedience to her charms. She blows a raging pestilence from her lips into the neighbouring folds; the innocent cattle die, to afford a fit sacrifice to the infernal deities. The moon, by powerful spells drawn down from her orb, enters the wood: legions of spirits from *Pluto*'s realms appear before the altar, and demand her pleasure. Tell me, said she, where I shall find what I have lost, my favourite little dog. How! cryed they all, enraged—Impertinent Beldame! must the order of nature be *inverted*, and the repose of every creature *disturbed*, for the sake of thy *little dog*?

FABLE III.

The Camelion.

TWO travellers happened on their journey to be engaged in a warm difpute about the *colour* of the Camelion. One of them affirmed it was *blue;* that he had feen it with his own eyes, upon the naked branch of a tree, feeding on *the air,* in a very clear day. The other ftrongly afferted it was *green,* and that he had viewed it very clofely and minutely on the *broad leaf* of a fig-tree. Both of them were pofitive, and the difpute was rifing to a quarrel: but a third perfon luckily coming by, they agreed to refer the queftion to his decifion. Gentlemen, faid the arbitrator with a fmile of great felf-fatisfaction, you could not have been more lucky in your reference, as I happen to have caught one of them laft *night:* but indeed you are both miftaken, for the creature is totally *black.* Black! impoffible! Nay, quoth the umpire, with great affurance; the matter may foon be decided, for I immediately enclofed my Camelion in a little *paper box,* and here it is. So faying, he drew it out of his pocket, opened his box, and behold, it was as *white* as fnow. The pofitive difputants looked equally furprifed, and equally confounded: while

the

the fagacious reptile, affuming the air of a philofopher, thus admonifhed them: Ye children of
men, learn *diffidence* and *moderation* in your opinions. 'Tis true, you happen, in this prefent
inftance, to be all in the right, and have only
confidered the fubject under different circumftances: but pray, for the future, allow others
to have *eye-fight* as well as yourfelves; nor wonder if every one prefers the teftimony of his *own*
fenfes, to that of *another's.*

F A B L E IV.

The Wolf and the Lamb.

A Flock of fheep were feeding in a meadow,
while their dogs were afleep, and their
fhepherd at a diftance, playing on his pipe, beneath the fhade of a fpreading elm. A young
unexperienced Lamb, obferving a half-ftarved
Wolf peeping through the pales of the enclofure,
entered into converfation with him. Pray, what
are you feeking for here? faid the Lamb. I am
looking, replied the Wolf, for fome tender grafs;
for nothing you know is more pleafant than to
feed in a frefh pafture, and to flake ones thirft
at a cryftal ftream: both which, I perceive, you
enjoy within thefe pales in their utmoft perfec-
tion. Happy creature! continued he, how much

J

I envy your lot! who are in full poffeffion of the utmoft I defire: for philofophy has long taught me to be fatisfied with a little. It feems then, returned the Lamb, thofe who fay you feed on flefh, accufe you falfely, fince a little grafs will eafily content you. If this be true, let us for the future live like brethren, and feed together. So faying, the fimple Lamb imprudently crept through the fence, and became at once a prey to our pretended philofopher, and a facrifice to his own inexperience and credulity.

FABLE V.

The Fox and the Bramble.

A Fox clofely purfued by a pack of dogs, took fhelter under the covert of a Bramble. He rejoiced in this afylum, and for a while was very happy: but foon found, that if he attempted to ftir, he was wounded by thorns and prickles on every fide. However, making a virtue of ne-ceffity, he forbore to complain; and comforted himfelf with reflecting, that *no blifs* is perfect; that *good* and *evil* are mixt, and flow from the *fame fountain.* Thefe briars indeed, faid he, will tear my fkin a little, yet they keep off the dogs. For the fake of the good then, let me bear the evil with patience; each bitter has its fweets, and

thefe

Plate 65.
1. The Miller, his Son, & their Ass.
2. The Sorceress.
3. The Camelion.
4. The Wolf & the Lamb.
5. The Fox & Bramble.
6. The Falcon and Hen.
7. The Travellers & Money bag.
8. The Discontented Ass.
9. The two Springs.
10. Rose and Butterfly.
11. The Tortoise & two Ducks.
12. The Cat and old Rat.

thefe Brambles though they wound my *flefh*, preferve my *life* from danger.

FABLE VI.

The Falcon and the Hen.

DIFFERENT circumftances make the *fame*
action right or wrong, a virtue or a vice.

Of all the creatures I ever knew, faid a Falcon to a Hen, you are certainly the moft un-
grateful. What inftance of ingratitude, replied
the Hen, can you juftly charge upon me? The
greateft, returned the Falcon; ingratitude to
your higheft benefactors, men. Do they not
feed you every day, and fhelter you every night?
Neverthelefs, when they endeavour to court you
to them, you ungratefully forget all their kind-
nefs, and fly from them as from an enemy. Now
I, who am wild by nature, and no way obliged
to them; yet upon the leaft of their careffes, fuffer myfelf to be taken, and go, or come at their
command. All this is very true, replied the
Hen, but there may be a fufficient reafon both
for *my fear*, and for *your familiarity:* I believe you
never faw a fingle Falcon *roafting* at the fire;
whereas I have feen an hundred Hens truffed
for *that* purpofe.

F

FABLE

FABLE VII.

The Travellers and the Money-bag.

AS two men were travelling on the road, one of them efpied a bag of Money lying on the ground. and picking it up, I am in luck this morning, faid he, I have found a Bag of Money. Yes, returned the other; though, methinks. you fhould not fay *I*, but *We* have found it: for when two friends are travelling together, they ought equally to fhare in any accidental good fortune that may happen to attend them. No, rejoined the former, it was I that *found* it, and I muft infift upon *keeping* it. He had no fooner fpoken the words than they were alarmed with a hue and cry after a thief, who had that morning taken a purfe upon the road. Lord, fays the finder, this is extremely unfortunate, *we* fhall certainly be feized. Good Sir, replied the other, be pleafed not to fay *We*, but *I*: as you would not allow me a fhare in the *prize*, you have no right to make me a partner in the *punifhment*.

FABLE VIII.

The difcontented Afs.

IN the depth of winter, a poor Afs prayed heartily for the fpring, that he might exchange a cold lodging, and a heartlefs trufs of ftraw, for a little warm weather and a mouthful of frefh gafs. In a fhort time, according to his wifh, the warm weather, and the frefh grafs came on; but brought with them fo much toil and bufinefs, that he was foon as weary of the fpring as before of the winter; and he now became impatient for the approach of fummer. Summer arrives: but the heat, the harveft-work, and other drudgeries and inconveniences of the feafon, fet him as far from happinefs as before; which he now flattered himfelf would be found in the plenty of autumn. But here too he is difappointed; for what with the carrying of apples, roots, fewel for the winter, and other provifions, he was in autumn more fatigued than ever. Having thus trod round the circle of the year, in a courfe of reftlefs labour, uneafinefs and difappointment; and found no feafon, nor ftation of life, without its bufinefs and its trouble; he was forced at laft to acquiefce in the *comfortlefs feafon* of winter, where his complaint

began :

began: convinced that in *this world*, every situation has its *inconvenience*.

FABLE IX.

The two Springs.

TWO Springs, which issued from the same fountain, began their course together: one of them took her way in a silent and gentle stream, while the other rushed along with a sounding and rapid current. Sister, said the latter, at the rate you move, you will probably be dried up before you advance much farther: whereas, for myself, I will venture a wager, that within two or three hundred furlongs I shall become navigable, and after distributing commerce and wealth wherever I flow, I shall majestically proceed to pay my tribute to the ocean: so farewel, dear sister, and patiently submit to your fate. Her sister made no reply; but calmly descending to the meadows below, increased her stream by numberless little rills, which she collected in her progress, till at length she was enabled to rise into a *considerable river*: whilst the proud Stream, who had the vanity to depend solely upon her own sufficiency, continued a *shallow brook*, and was glad at last to be helped forward, by throwing herself into the arms of her despised sister.

FABLE

FABLE X.

The Rose and the Butterfly.

A Fine powdered Butterfly fell in love with a beautiful Rose, who expanded her charms in a neighbouring parterre. Matters were soon adjusted between them, and they mutually vowed eternal fidelity. The Butterfly, perfectly satisfied with the success of his amour, took a tender leave of his mistress, and did not return again till noon. What! said the Rose, when she saw him approach, is the ardent passion you vowed, so soon extinguished? It is an age since you paid me a visit. But no wonder: for I observed you courting by turns every flower in the garden. You little coquet, replied the Butterfly, it well becomes *you* truely, to reproach me with my gallantries; when in fact I only copy the example which *you yourself* have set me. For, not to mention the satisfaction with which you admitted the kiss of the fragrant Zephyr; did I not see you displaying your charms to the *bee*, the *fly*, the *wasp*, and in short, encouraging and receiving the addresses of every buzzing insect that fluttered within your view? If *you* will be a coquet, you must expect to find *me* inconstant.

F 3

FABLE

FABLE XI.

The Tortoise and two Ducks.

VANITY and idle curiofity are qualities which generally prove deftructive to thofe who fuffer themfelves to be governed by them.

A Tortoife, weary of paffing her days in the fame obfcure corner, conceived a wonderful inclination to vifit foreign countries. Two Ducks, whom the fimple Tortoife acquainted with her intention, undertook to oblige her upon the occafion. Accordingly they told her, that if fhe would faften her mouth to the middle of a pole, they would take the two ends, and tranfport her whitherfoever fhe chofe to be conveyed. The Tortoife approved of the expedient; and every thing being prepared, the Ducks began their flight with her. They had not travelled far in the air, when they were met by a crow, who enquiring what they were bearing along, they replied, The *queen* of the Tortoifes. The Tortoife, vain of the new and unmerited appellation, was going to *confirm* the title, when opening her mouth for that purpofe, fhe let go her hold, and was dafhed to pieces by her fall.

FABLE

FABLE XII.

The Cat and the old Rat.

A Certain Cat had made such unmerciful havoc among the vermin of her neighbourhood, that not a single Rat or Mouse dared venture to appear abroad. Puss was soon convinced, that if affairs remained in their present situation, she must be totally unsupplied with provision. After mature deliberation therefore, she resolved to have recouse to stratagem. For this purpose, she suspended herself from a hook with her head downwards, pretending to be dead. The rats and mice observing her, as they peeped from their holes, in this dangling attitude, concluded she was hanged for some misdemeanour; and with great joy immediately sallied forth in quest of their prey. Puss, as soon as a sufficient number were collected together, quitting her hold, dropped into the midst of them; and very few had the fortune to make good their retreat. *This* artifice having succeeded so well, she was encouraged to try the event of a *second.* Accordingly she whitened her coat all over, by rolling herself in a heap of flour, and in this disguise lay concealed in the bottom of a meal tub. This stratagem was executed, in general, with the same

F 4

effect

effect as the former. But an old experienced Rat, altogether as cunning as his adversary, was not so easily ensnared. I don't much like, said he, that white heap yonder; something whispers me, there is mischief concealed under it. 'Tis true. it may be meal; but it may likewise be something that I shall not relish quite so well. There can be no harm, at least, in keeping at a proper distance: for *caution*, I am sure, is the parent of *security*.

F A B L E XIII.

The Country Maid and her Milk-pail

WHEN men suffer their imaginations to amuse them with the prospect of distant and uncertain improvements of their condition; they frequently sustain real losses. by their inattention to those affairs in which they are immediately concerned.

A Country Maid was walking very deliberately with a Pail of Milk upon her head, when she fell into the following train of reflections. The money, for which I shall sell this Milk, will enable me to increase my flock of eggs to three hundred. These eggs. allowing for what may prove addle, and what may be destroyed by vermin,

min, will produce at leaft. two hundred and
fifty chickens. The chickens will be fit to carry
to market about Chriftmas, when poultry always
bear a good price: fo that by May-day, I cannot fail of having money enough to purchafe a
new gown. Green—let me confider.—yes, green
becomes my complexion beft, and green it fhall
be. In this drefs I will go to the fair, where all
the young fellows will ftrive to have me for a
partner: but I fhall perhaps refufe every one of
them, and with an air of difdain *tofs* from them
—Tranfported with this triumphant thought, fhe
could not forbear acting with her *head*, what thus
paffed in her *imagination;* when down came the
Pail of Milk, and all her *imaginary happinefs* va-
nifhed in a moment.

F A B L E XIV.

The Cormorant and the Fifhes.

IT is very imprudent to truft an enemy, or even
a ftranger, fo far as to put one's felf in his
power.

A Cormorant whofe eyes were become fo dim
by age, that he could not difcern his prey at
the bottom of the waters, bethought himfelf of
a ftratagem to fupply his wants. Hark you, friend,
faid

said he to a Gudgeon, whom he observed swimming near the surface of a certain canal, if you have any regard for yourself or your brethren, go this moment and acquaint them from me, that the owner of this piece of water is determined to drag it a week hence. The Gudgeon immediately swam away, and made his report of this terrible news to a general assembly of the Fishes; who unanimously agreed to send him back as their embassador to the Cormorant. The purport of his commission was to return him their thanks for the intelligence; and to add their intreaties, that, as he had been so good as to inform them of their danger, he would be graciously pleased to put them into a method of escaping it. That I will most readily, returned the artful Cormorant, and assist you with my best services into the bargain. You have only to collect yourselves together at the top of the water, and I will undertake to transport you one by one to my *own refidence*, by the side of a folitary pool, to which no creature but myself ever found the way. The project was perfectly well approved by the *unwary* Fishes, and with great expedition performed by the *deceitful* Cormorant; who having placed them in a shallow water, the bottom of which his eye could easily discern,

they

they were all devoured by him in their turns, as his *hunger* or *luxury* required.

FABLE XV.

The Athiest and the Acorn.

IT was the fool who said in his heart, *There is no God:* into the breast of a wise man, such a thought could never have entered. One of those refined Reasoners, commonly called Minute Philosophers, was sitting at his ease beneath the shade of a large oak, while at his side the weak branches of a pumpion were trailed upon the ground. This threw our great logician into his old track of reasoning against providence. Is it consistent with *common sense*, said he, that *infinite wisdom* should create so large and stately a tree, with branches of such *prodigious* strength, only to bear so small and insignificant a fruit as an *Acorn?* Or that so weak a stem, as that of a pumpion, should be loaded with so disproportioned a weight? A child may see the absurdity of it. In the midst of this curious speculation, down dropt an Acorn, from one of the highest branches of the oak, full upon his head. How small a trifle may overturn the systems of *mighty philosophers!* Struck with the accident, he could not help crying out, How *providential* it is that this was not a pumpion!

FABLE XVI.

The Lynx and the Mole.

UNDER the covert of a thick wood, at the foot of a tree, as a Lynx lay whetting his teeth, and waiting for his prey; he efpied a Mole, half buried under a hilloc of her own raifing. Alas, poor creature, faid the Lynx, how much I pity thee! Surely Jupiter has been very unkind, to debar thee from the light of the day, which rejoices the whole creation. Thou art certainly not above half alive; and it would be doing thee a fervice, to put an end to fo un-animated a being. I thank you for your kind-nefs, replied the Mole, but I think I have full as much vivacity, as my ftate and circumftances require. For the reft, I am perfectly well con-tented with the faculties which Jupiter has al-lotted me, who I am fure wants not our direc-tion in diftributing his gifts with *propriety*. I have not, 'tis true, your piercing eyes; but I have ears which anfwer all my purpofes full as well. Hark! for example, I am warned, by a noife which I hear behind you, to fly from dan-ger. So faying, he flunk into the earth; while

a javelin from the arm of a hunter, pierced the
quick-fighted Lynx to the heart.

F A B L E   XVII.

The Spider and the Silk-worm.

THOSE arts are moſt valuable, which are
of greateſt uſe.

A Spider, buſied in ſpreading his web from
one ſide of a room to the other, was aſked by
an induſtrious Silk-worm, to what end he ſpent
ſo much time and labour, in making ſuch a
number of lines and circles? The Spider angrily
replied, Do not diſturb me, thou ignorant thing:
I tranſmit my ingenuity to *poſterity*, and *fame* is
the objeſt of my wiſhes. Juſt as he had ſpoken,
Suſan the chambermaid, coming into the room
to feed her Silk-worms, faw the ſpider at his
work; and with one ſtroke of her broom, ſwept
him away, and deſtroyed at once his *labours*, and
hopes of *fame*.

FABLE XVIII.

The Bee and the Fly.

A Bee obferving a Fly frifking about her hive, afked him in a very paffionate tone, what he did there? Is it for fuch fcoundrels as you, faid fhe, to intrude into the company of the queens of the air? You have great reafon truly, replied the Fly, to be out of humour: I am fure they muft be mad, who would have any concern with fo quarrelfome a nation. And why fo? thou faucy malapert, returned the enraged Bee: we have the beft laws, and are governed by the beft policy in the world. We feed upon the moft fragrant flowers, and all our bufinefs is to make honey? honey, which equals nectar, thou taftelefs wretch, who liveft upon nothing but putrefaction and excrement. We live as we can, rejoined the Fly: poverty, I hope, is no crime; but paffion *is one*, I am fure. The honey you make, is fweet I grant you; but your heart is all bitternefs: for to be revenged on an enemy, you'll deftroy your own life; and are fo inconfiderate in your rage, as to do more mifchief to yourfelf, than to your adverfary. Take my word for it, one had better have *lefs* confiderable talents, and ufe them with *more* difcretion.

FABLE XIX.

Genius, Virtue, and Reputation.

GENIUS, Virtue, and Reputation, three intimate friends, agreed to travel over the ifland of Great Breton, to fee whatever might be worthy of obfervation. But as fome misfortune, faid they, may happen to feparate us; let us confider before we fet out, by what means we may find each other again. Should it be my ill fate, faid Genius, to be fevered from my friends, which heaven forbid! you may find me kneeling in devotion before the tomb of Shakefpear; or rapt in fome grove where Milton talked with angels; or mufing in the grotto where Pope caught infpiration. Virtue, with a figh, acknowledged that her friends were not very numerous: but were I to lofe you, fhe cryed, with whom I am at prefent fo happily united; I fhould chufe to take fanctuary in the temples of religion, in the palaces of royalty, or in the ftately domes of minifters of ftate: but as it may be my ill fortune to be *there* denied admittance, enquire for fome cottage where *Contentment* has a bower, and there you will *certainly* find me. Ah, my dear companions, faid Reputation very earneftly, you I perceive, when miffing, may poffibly

be

be recovered; but take care, I intreat you, always to keep fight of me, for if I am *once loft*, I am *never to be retrieved.*

FABLE XX.

The Court of Death.

DEATH, the king of terrors, on the anniverfary of his coronation, was determined to chufe his prime minifter. His pale courtiers, the ghaftly train of difeafes, were all fummoned to attend: when each preferred his claim to the honour of this illuftrious office. Fever urged the numbers he deftroyed; cold Palfy fet forth his pretentions, by fhaking all his limbs; and Dropfy, by his fwelled unwieldly carcafe. Gout hobbled up, and alledged his great power in racking every joint; and Afthma's inability to fpeak, was a ftrong, though filent argument in favour of his claim. Stone and Cholic pleaded their violence; Plague, his rapid progrefs in defluction; and Confumption tho' flow, infifted that he was fure. In the midft of this contention, the court was difturbed with the noife of mufic, dancing, feafting, and revelry; when immediately entered a lady with a bold lafcivious air, and a flufhed and jovial countenance: fhe was attended on one hand by a troop of cooks and

bacchanals;

13 Country Maid
and her Milk.
14 Cormorant
and Fishes.
15 The Atheist
and the Acorn.
16 The Lyon
and the Mole.
17 The Spider
& Silkworm.
18 The Bee
and Fly.
19 Genius, Virtue,
& Reputation.
20 The Court
of Death.
21 Industry
and Sloth.
22 The
Hare's Ears.
23 The Hermit
and the Bear.
24 The Passen-
ger & Pilot.

bacchanals; and on the other by a train of wanton youths and damsels, who danced half naked to the softest musical instruments; her name was INTEMPERANCE. She waved her hand, and thus addressed the crowd of Diseases. Give way, ye sickly band of pretenders, nor dare to vie with my superior merits in the service of this great Monarch. Am not I your *parent?* the author of your *beings?* Do you not derive your power of shortening human life almost wholly from me? Who then so fit as myself for this important office? The grisly Monarch grinned a smile of approbation, placed her at his right hand, and she immediately became his *prime* favourite, and *principal* minister.

FABLE XXI.

Industry and Sloth.

HOW many live in the world as useless, as if they had never been born! They pass through life, like a bird through the air, and leave no track behind them: waste the prime of their days in *deliberating* what they shall do; and bringing them to a period, without coming to any *determination*.

An

An indolent young man, being asked why he lay in bed so long, jocosely and carelessly answered—Every morning of my life I am hearing causes, I have two fine girls, their names are Industry and Sloth, close at my bed side, as soon as ever I awake, pressing their different suits. One intreats me to get up, the other persuades me to lie still: and then they alternately give me various reasons, why I should rise, and why I should not. This detains me so long, as it is the duty of an impartial judge to hear all that can be said on either side, that before the pleadings are over, it is time to go to dinner.

FABLE XXII.

The Hare's Ears.

AN Elk having accidently gored a Lion, the monarch was so exasperated, that he sent forth an edict, commanding all horned beasts, on pain of death, to depart his dominions. A Hare observing the shadow of her Ears, was much alarmed at their long and lofty apperance; and running to one of her friends, acquainted him that she was resolved to quit the country. For should I happen, said she, however undesignedly, to give offence to my superiors, my Ears may be construed to come within the horn-act.

Her

Her friend smiled at her apprehensions: and asked, how it was possible that Ears could be mistaken for horns? Had I no more Ears than an ostrich, replied the Hare, I would not trust them in the hands of an informer: for *truth* and *innocence* are arguments of little force, against the *logic of power* and *malice* in conjunction.

FABLE XXIII.

The Hermit and the Bear.

AN imprudent friend often does as much mischief by his *too great zeal*, as the worst enemy could effect by his *malice*.

A certain Hermit having done a good office to a Bear, the grateful creature was so sensible of his obligation, that he begged to be admitted as the guardian and companion of his solitude. The Hermit willingly accepted his offer; and conducted him to his cell, where they passed their time together in an amicable manner. One very hot day, the Hermit having laid him down to sleep, the officious Bear employed himself in driving away the flies from his *patron's* face. But in spite of all his care, one of the flies perpetually returned to the attack, and at last, settled upon the Hermit's nose. Now I shall have you most

certainly.

certainly, faid the Bear; and with the beft intentions imaginable, gave him a violent blow on
the face; which very effectually indeed demolifhed the fly, but at the fame time moft terribly
bruifed the face of his benefactor.

FABLE XXIV.

The Paffenger and the Pilot.

IT had blown a violent ftorm at fea, and the
whole crew of a veffel were in imminent danger of fhipwreck. After the rolling of the waves
was fomewhat abated, a certain Paffenger who
had never been at fea before, obferving the Pilot to have appeared wholly unconcerned, even
in their greateft danger, had the curiofity to afk
him what death his father died. What death?
faid the Pilot; why he perifhed at fea, as my
grandfather did before him. And are not you
afraid of trufting yourfelf to an element that has
proved thus fatal to your family? Afraid! by
no means; why, we muft all die: is not your
father dead? Yes, but he died in his bed. And
why then are not you afraid of trufting yourfelf
to your bed? Becaufe I am there perfectly fecure. It may be fo, replied the Pilot; but if
the hand of providence is equally extended over
all places, there is no more reafon for *me* to be
afraid

afraid of going to *sea*, than for *you* to be afraid of going to *bed*.

FABLE XXV.

The partial Judge.

A Farmer came to a neighbouring Lawyer, expressing great concern for an accident which he said had just happened. One of your oxen, continued he, has been gored by an unlucky bull of mine, and I should be glad to know how I am to make you reparation. Thou art a very honest fellow, replied the Lawyer, and wilt not think it unreasonable, that I expect one of thy oxen in return. It is no more than justice, quoth the Farmer, to be sure: but what did I say?—I mistake—It is *your* bull that has killed one of *my* oxen. Indeed! says the Lawyer, that alters the case: I must enquire into the affair; and if—And *if!* said the Farmer—the business I find would have been concluded without an *if;* had you been as ready to do justice to others, as to exact it from them.

FABLE XXVI.

The Fox that had loſt his Tail.

A Fox having been unwarily caught in a trap, with much ſtrugling and difficulty, at length diſengaged himſelf; not however without being obliged to leave his Tail behind him. The joy he felt at his eſcape, was ſomewhat abated when he began to conſider the price he had paid for it: and he was a good deal mortified by reflecting on the ridiculous figure he ſhould make among his brethren, without a Tail. In the agitation of his thoughts upon this occaſion, an expedient occurred to him, which he reſolved to try, in order to remove this diſgraceful ſingularity. With this view he aſſembled his tribe together, and ſet forth in a moſt elaborate ſpeech, how much he had at heart, whatever tended to the public weal: he had often thought, he ſaid, on the length and buſhineſs of their Tails; was verily perſuaded that it was much more burthenſome, than ornamental, and rendered them beſides an eaſier prey to their enemies. He earneſtly recommended it to them, therefore, to diſcharge themſelves of ſo *uſeleſs* and *dangerous* an incumbrance. My good friend, replied an old Fox, who had liſtened very attentively to

his

his harangue, we are much obliged to you, no doubt, for the concern you exprefs upon our account: but pray turn about before the company, for I cannot, for my life, help fufpecting, that you would not be quite fo follicitous to eafe us of *our* Tails, if you had not unluckily loft *your own.*

F A B L E XXVII.

The Nobleman and his Son.

A Certain Nobleman, much infected by fuperftition, dreamed one night that his only Son, a youth about fifteen years of age, was thrown from his horfe as he was hunting, and killed upon the fpot. This idle dream made fo ftrong an impreffion upon the weak and credulous father. that he formed a refolution never more to fuffer his Son to partake of this his favourite diverfion. The next morning that the hounds went out, the young man requefted permiffion to follow them; but inftead of receiving it, as ufual, his father acquainted him with his dream, and peremptorily enjoined him to forbear the fport. The youth, greatly mortified at this unexpected refufal, left the room much difconcerted, and it was with fome difficulty that he reftrained his paffion from indecently breaking out in his father's prefence. But upon his

G 4

return

return to his own apartment. paffing through a
gallery of pictures, in which was a piece repre-
fenting a company of gypfies telling a country
girl her fortune.—'Tis owing, faid he, to a ridiculous fuperftition of the fame kind, with that
of this fimple wench, that I am debarred from
one of the principal pleafures of my life : at the
fame time, with great emotion, he ftruck his
hand againft the canvas ; when a rufty old nail,
behind the picture, ran far into his wrift. The
pain and anguifh of the wound threw the youth
into a violent fever, which proved too powerful
for the fkill of the phyficians, and in a few days
put an end to his life : illuftrating an obfervation, that an over-cautious attention to *avoid*
evils, often brings them *upon* us ; and that we
are frequently thrown headlong *into misfortunes*,
by the very means we make ufe of to *avoid them*.

F A B L E   XXVIII.

Jupiter and the Herdfman.

A Herdfman miffed a young heifer out of his
grounds, and, after having diligently fought
for it in vain, when he could by no other means
gain intelligence of it, betook himfelf at laft to
his prayers. Great Jupiter, faid he, fhew me
but the villain who has done me this injury, and

I

I will give thee in facrifice the fineft kid from
my flock. He had no fooner uttered his petition, than turning the corner of a wood. he was
ftruck with the fight of a monftrous lion, prey-
ing on the carcafe of his heifer. Trembling and
pale, O Jupiter, cried he, I offered thee a kid
if thou wouldft *grant my petition:* I now offer thee
a bull, if thou wilt deliver me from the *confequence of it.*

F A B L E   XXIX.

The Eagle and the Owl.

AN Eagle and an Owl having entered into a
league of mutual amity, one of the articles
of their treaty was, that the former fhould not
prey upon the younglings of the latter. But tell
me, faid the Owl, fhould you know my little
ones, if you were to fee them? Indeed I fhould
not, replied the Eagle; but if you defcribe them
to me, it will be fufficient. You are to obferve
then, returned the Owl, in the firft place, that
the charming creatures are perfectly well-fhaped;
in the next, that there is a remarkable fweetnefs
and vivacity in their countenances; and then
there is fomething in their voices fo peculiarly
melodious—'Tis enough, interrupted the Eagle;
by thefe marks I cannot fail of diftinguifhing
them:

them: and you may depend upon their never receiving any injury from me. It happened not long afterwards, as the Eagle was upon the wing in queſt of his prey, that he diſcovered amidſt the ruins of an old caſtle, a neſt of grim-faced, ugly birds, with gloomy countenances, and a voice like that of the furies. Theſe undoubtedly, ſaid he, cannot be the offspring of my friend, and ſo I ſhall venture to make free with them. He had ſcarce finiſhed his repaſt and departed, when the Owl returned; who, finding nothing of her brood remaining but ſome fragments of the mangled carcaſes, broke out into the moſt bitter exclamations againſt the cruel and perfidious author of her calamity. A neighbouring bat, who over-heard her lamentations, and had been witneſs to what had paſſed between her and the Eagle; very gravely told her, that ſhe had nobody to blame for this misfortune, but herſelf: whoſe blind prejudices in favour of her children, had prompted her to give ſuch a deſcription of them, as did not reſemble them in any one ſingle feature or quality.

Parents ſhould very carefully guard againſt that weak partiality towards their children, which renders them blind to their failings and imper-

fections:

fections: as no difposition is more likely to prove prejudicial to their future welfare.

F A B L E XXX.

The Plague among the Beaſts.

A Mortal diſtemper once raged among the Beaſts, and fwept away prodigious numbers. After it had continued fome time without abatement, it was concluded in an aſſembly of the brute creation to be a judgment inflicted upon them for their fins, and a day was appointed for a general confeſſion; when it was agreed, that he who appeared to be the greateſt finner, ſhould fuffer death, as an atonement for the reft. The Fox was appointed father confeſſor upon the occaſion; and the Lion with great generoſity, condeſcended to be the firſt in making public confeſſion. For my part, faid he, I muſt own I have been an enormous offender; I have killed many *innocent ſheep* in my time; nay once, but it was a cafe of neceſſity, I made a meal of the *ſhepherd.* the Fox, with much gravity, acknowledged, that thefe in any other than the King, would have been *inexpiable crimes;* but that his majeſty had certainly a *right* to a few filly ſheep, nay, and to the ſhepherd too, in cafe of neceſſity. The judgment of the Fox was applauded

by

by all the superior savages; and the Tyger, the Leopard, the Bear, and the Wolf, made confession of many enormities of the like sanguinary nature: which were all palliated or excused with the same lenity and mercy; and their crimes accounted so venial, as scarce to deserve the name of offences. At last, a poor penitent Ass, with great contrition acknowledged, that once going through the parson's meadow, being very hungry, and tempted by the sweetness of the grass, he had cropt a little of it, not more however in quantity, than the tip of his tongue: he was very sorry for the misdemeanour, and hoped—Hope! exclaimed the Fox with singular zeal, what canst thou hope for, after the commission of so heinous a crime? What! eat the parson's grass! O sacrilege! This, this is the flagrant wickedness, my brethren, which has drawn the wrath of heaven upon our heads, and this the notorious offender, whose death must make atonement for all our transgressions. So saying, he ordered his entrails for sacrifice, and the rest of the Beasts went to dinner upon his carcase.

FABLE XXXI.

The Cat, the Cock, and the young Mouse.

A Young Mouſe, who had ſeen very little of the world, came running one day to his mother in great haſte—O mother, ſaid he, I am frighted almoſt to death! I have ſeen the moſt extraordinary creature that ever was. He has a fierce angry look, and ſtruts about upon two legs. A ſtrange piece of fleſh grows upon his head, and another under his throat, as red as blood. He flapped his arms againſt his ſides, as if he intended to riſe into the air; and ſtretching out his head, he opened a ſharppointed mouth ſo wide, that I thought he was preparing to ſwallow me up: then he roared at me ſo horribly, that I trembled every joint, and was glad to run home as faſt as I could. If I had not been frightened away by this terrible monſter, I was juſt going to ſcrape acquaintance with the prettieſt creature you ever ſaw. She had a ſoft furr ſkin, thicker than ours, and all beautifully ſtreaked with black and grey; with a modeſt look, and a demeanour ſo humble and courteous, that methought I could have fallen in love with her. Then ſhe had a fine long tail, which ſhe waved about ſo prettily, and looked ſo earneſtly at me, that

J

I do believe she was just going to speak to me,
when the horrid monster frightened me away.
Ah, my dear child, said the mother, you have
escaped being devoured, but not by that monster
you was so much afraid of: which in truth was
only a bird, and would have done you no manner of harm. Whereas the sweet creature, of
whom you seem so fond, was no other, than a
Cat; who, under that *hypocritical* countenance,
conceals the most *inveterate hatred* to all our race,
and subsists entirely by devouring Mice. Learn
from this incident, my dear, never whilst you
live to *rely on outward appearances.*

F A B L E XXXII.

The Farmer and his Dog.

A Farmer who had just stepped into his field
to mend a gap in one of his fences, found
at his return, the cradle, where he had left his
only child asleep, turned upside down, the clothes
all torn and bloody, and his Dog lying near it
besmeared also with blood. Immediately conceiving that the creature had destroyed his child,
he instantly dashed out his brains with the hatchet
in his hand: when turning up the cradle, he
found his child unhurt, and an enormous serpent
lying dead on the floor, killed by that faithful

Dog,

25 The partial Judge.

26 Fox that had lost his tail.

27 Nobleman & his Son.

28 Jupiter and y. Herdsman.

29 The Eagle & Owl.

30 The Plague among y. Beasts

31 The Cat, y. Cock, & young Mouse.

32 The Farmer & his Dog.

33 The Gnat & the Bee.

34 The Owl & the Eagle.

35 Sick Lion, Fox, and Wolf.

36 Blind man and Lame.

Dog, whofe courage and fidelity in preferving the life of his fon, deferved another kind of reward. Thefe affecting circumftances afforded him a ftriking leffon, how dangerous it is too *haftily* to give way to the blind impulfe of a *fudden paffion*.

F A B L E XXXIII.

The Gnat and the Bee.

A Gnat half ftarved with cold, and pinched with hunger, came early one morning to a Bee-hive, begging the relief of charity, and offered to teach mufic in the family, on the humble terms of diet and lodging. The Bee received her petitioner with a cold civility, and defired to be excufed. I bring up all my children, faid fhe, to my own ufual trade. that they may be able when they grow up, to get an honeft livelihood by their induftry. Befides, how do you think I could be fo imprudent as to teach them an art, which I fee has reduced its Profeffor to indigence and beggary?

FABLE XXXIV.

The Owl and the Eagle.

AN Owl fate blinking in the trunk of a hollow tree. and arraigned the brightnefs of the fun. What is the ufe of its beams, faid fhe, but to dazzle ones eyes fo that one cannot fee a moufe? For my part, I am at a lofs to conceive for what purpofe fo glaring an objeƈt was created. We had certainly been much better without it. O fool! replied an Eagle perched on a branch of the fame tree, to rail at excellence which thou canft not tafte; and not to perceive that the fault is not in the fun, but in thyfelf. All, 'tis true, have not faculties to underftand, or powers to enjoy the benefit of it; but muft the *bufinefs* and the *pleafures* of the world be obftruƈted, that an Owl may *catch mice?*

FABLE XXXV.

The fick Lion, the Fox, and the Wolf.

A Lion, having furfeited himfelf with feafting too luxurioufly on the carcafe of a wild boar. was feized with a violent and dangerous diforder. The beafts of the foreft fiocked in great numbers to pay their refpeƈts to him upon the occafion,

and

and fcarce one was abfent except the Fox. The Wolf, an illnatured and malicious beaft, feized this opportunity to accufe the Fox of pride, ingratitude, and difaffection to his majefty. In the midft of his invective, the Fox entered; who having heard part of the Wolf's accufation, and obferving the Lion's countenance to be kindling into wrath, thus adroitly excufed himfelf, and retorted upon his accufer. With a tone of zealous loyalty he addreffed the affembly thus: May the King live for ever! then turning to the Lion —I fee many here, who, with mere lip-fervice, have pretended to fhew you their loyalty: but for my part. from the moment I heard of your majefty's illnefs, neglecting ufelefs compliments. I employed myfelf day and night to enquire among the moft learned phyficians, an infallable remedy for your difeafe, and have at length happily been informed of one. It is a plaifter made from part of the fkin of a Wolf, taken warm from his back, and laid to your majefty's ftomach. This remedy was no fooner propofed, than it was determined that the experiment fhould be tried: and whilft the operation was performing; the Fox, with a farcaftic fmile, whifpered this ufeful maxim in the Wolf's ear—If you would be *fafe from harm yourfelf,* learn for the future, *not to meditate mifchief againft others.*

H

F A B L E

FABLE XXXVI.

The Blind Man and the Lame.

'TIS from our wants and infirmities that almoſt all the connections of ſociety take
their riſe.

A Blind Man, being ſtopped in a bad piece of
road, meets with a Lame Man, and intreats him
to guide him through the difficulty he was got
into. How can I do that, replied the Lame Man,
ſince I am ſcarce able to drag myſelf along? but
as you appear to be very ſtrong, if you will carry
me, we will ſeek our fortunes together. It will
then be my intereſt to warn you of any thing
that may obſtruct your way: your feet ſhall be
my feet, and my eyes yours. With all my heart,
returned the Blind Man; let us render each other
our mutual ſervices. So taking his lame companion on his back, they by means of their union, travelled on with ſafety and pleaſure.

FABLE XXXVII.

The Lion, the Bear, the Monkey, and the Fox.

THE Tyrant of the foreſt iſſued a proclama-
tion, commanding all his ſubjects to repair
immediately to his royal den.   Among the reſt,
the Bear made his appearance: but pretending
to be offended with the ſteams which iſſued from
the monarch's apartment, he was imprudent
enough to *hold his noſe* in his majeſty's preſence.
This inſolence was ſo highly reſented, that the
Lion in a rage laid him dead at his feet.   The
Monkey, obſerving what had paſſed, trembled
for his carcaſe; and attempted to conciliate favour by the moſt abject flattery. He began with
proteſting, that for his part, he thought the
apartments were perfumed with Arabian ſpices;
and exclaiming againſt the rudeneſs of the Bear,
admired the *beauty* of his majeſty's paws, ſo *happily formed*, he ſaid, to correct the inſolence of
clowns. This fulſome adulation, inſtead of being
received as he expected, proved no leſs offenſive,
than the rudeneſs of the Bear: and the courtly
Monkey was in like manner extended by the
ſide of Sir Bruin. And now his majeſty caſt his
eye upon the Fox. Well, Reynard, ſaid he, and
what ſcent do you diſcover here? Great prince,

                    replied

replied the cautious Fox, *my nose* was never esteemed my most *distinguishing sense*: and at present I would by no means venture to give my opinion, as I have unfortunately got a *terrible cold*.

FABLE XXXVIII.

The Owl and the Nightingale.

A Formal solemn Owl had many years made his habitation in a grove amongst the ruins of an old monastery, and had pored so often on some mouldy manuscripts, the stupid relicks of a monkish library, that he grew infected with the pride and pedantry of the place; and mistaking gravity for wisdom, would sit whole days with his eyes half shut, fancying himself profoundly learned. It happened, as he sate one evening, half buried in meditation, and half in sleep, that a Nightingale, unluckily perching near him, began her melodious lays. He started from his *reverie,* and with a horrid screech interrupted her song—Be gone, cried he, thou impertinent minstrel, nor distract with noisy dissonance, my sublime contemplations; and know, vain songster, that harmony consists in truth alone, which is gained by laborious study; and not in languishing notes, fit only to sooth the ear of a love-sick maid. Conceited pedant! returned

turned the Nightingale, whose wisdom lies only
in the feathers that muffle up thy unmeaning
face; music is a natural and rational entertainment, and though not adapted to the ears of an
Owl, has ever been relished and admired by all
who are possessed of true taste and elegance.

FABLE XXXIX.

The Ant and the Caterpillar.

AS a Caterpillar was advancing very slowly
along one of the alleys of a beautiful garden, he was met by a pert lively Ant, who toss-
ing up her head with a scornful air, cried, prithee
get out of the way, thou poor creeping animal,
and do not presume to obstruct the paths of thy
superiors, by wriggling along the road, and be-
smearing the walks appropriated to their foot-
steps. Poor creature! thou lookest like a thing
half made, which nature, not liking, threw by un-
finished. I could almost pity thee, methinks;
but it is beneath one of my quality to talk to
such little mean creatures as thou art: and so,
poor crawling wretch, adieu.

The humble Caterpillar struck dumb with this
disdainful language, retired, went to work, wound
himself up in a silken cell, and at the appointed

H 3

time

time came out a beautiful Butterfly. Juft as he was iffuing forth, he obferved the fcornful Ant paffing by. Proud infect, faid he, ftop a moment, and liften to what I fhall fay. Let me advife you never to *defpife* any one for his *condition*, as there are none fo mean, but they may one day *change their fortune.* You behold me now *exalted* in the *air,* whereas you muft *creep* as long as you live.

F A B L E XL.

The two Foxes.

TWO Foxes formed a ftratagem to enter a hen-rooft: which having fuccefsfully executed, and killed the cock, the hens, and the chickens, they began to feed upon them with fingular fatisfaction. One of the Foxes, who was young and inconfiderate, was for devouring them all *upon the fpot:* the other, who was old and covetous, propofed to referve fome of them for *another time.* "For experience, child, faid he, has made me wife, and I have feen many unexpected events fince I came into the world. Let us provide, therefore, againft what may happen, and not confume all our ftores at one *meal.*" "All this is wonderous wife, replied the young Fox; but for my part, I am refolved not to ftir

till

till I have eaten as much as will ferve me a whole week: for who would be mad enough to return hither? when it is certain the owner of thefe fowls will watch for us, and if he fhould catch us, would certainly put us to death." After this fhort difcourfe, each purfued his own fcheme: the young Fox eat till he burft himfelf, and had fcarcely ftrength to reach his hole before he died. The old one, who thought it much better to deny his appetite for the prefent, and lay up provifion for the future, returned the next day, and was killed by the farmer. Thus *every age* has its *peculiar vice:* the young fuffer by their infatiable thirft after *pleafure;* and the old, by their incorrigible and inordinate *avarice.*

F A B L E XLI.

The conceited Owl.

A Young Owl having accidentally feen himfelf in a cryftal fountain, conceived the higheft opinion of his perfonal perfections. 'Tis time, faid he, that Hymen fhould give me children as beautiful as myfelf, to be the glory of the night, and the ornament of our groves. What pity would it be, if the race of the moft accomplifhed of birds fhould be extinct for my want of a mate! Happy the female who is deftined to

H 4

fpend

fpend her life with me! Full of thefe felf-approving thoughts, he intreated the Crow to propofe a match between him and the royal daughter of the Eagle. Do you imagine, faid the Crow, that the noble Eagle, whofe *pride* it is to *gaze* on the brighteft of the heavenly luminaries, will confent to marry his daughter to you, who cannot fo much as *open your eyes* whilft it is *day-light?* But the felf-conceited Owl was deaf to all that his friend could urge; who after much perfuafion, was at length prevailed upon to undertake the commiffion. His propofal was received in the manner that might be expected: the king of birds laughed him to fcorn. However, being a monarch of fome humour, he ordered him to acquaint the Owl, that if he would meet him the next morning at fun-rife in the middle of the fky, he would confent to give him his daughter in marriage. The prefumptuous Owl undertook to perform the condition; but being dazzled with the fun, and his head growing giddy, he fell from his height upon a rock; from whence being purfued by a flight of birds, he was glad at laft to make his efcape into the hollow of an old oak; where he paffed the remainder of his days in that obfcurity, for which nature defigned him.

FABLE

FABLE XLII.

The Fox and the Cat.

NOTHING is more common than for men to condemn the very same actions in others, which they practise themselves whenever occasion offers.

A Fox and a Cat having made a party to travel together, beguiled the tediousness of their journey by a variety of philosophical conversations. Of all the moral virtues, exclaimed Reynard, mercy is sure the noblest! What say you, my sage friend, is it not so? Undoubtedly, replied the Cat, with a most demure countenance; nothing is more becoming, in a creature of any sensibility, than a compassionate disposition. While they were thus *moralizing*, and mutually complimenting each other on the wisdom of their respective reflections; a Wolf darted out, from a wood, upon a flock of sheep which were feeding in an adjacent meadow; and without being in the least affected by the *moving lamentations* of a poor lamb, devoured it before their eyes. *Horrible cruelty!* exclaimed the Cat; why does he not feed on *vermin*, instead of making his barbarous

meals

meals on such *innocent creatures?* Reynard agreed with his friend in the obfervation: to which he added feveral very pathetic remarks on the odiouf-nefs of a *fanguinary temper.* Their indignation was rifing in its warmth and zeal, when they arrived at a little cottage by the way-fide; where the tender-hearted Reynard immediately caft his eye upon a fine cock that was ftruting about in the yard. And now, *adieu moralizing :* he leaped over the pales, and without any fort of fcruple demolifhed his prize in an inftant. In the mean while, a plump moufe which ran out of the fta-ble, totally put to flight our Cat's philofophy, who fell to the repaft without the leaft commife-ration.

F A B L E XLIII.

The two Horfes.

TWO Horfes were travelling the road toge-ther; one loaded with a fack of flour, the other with a fum of money. The latter, proud of his fplendid burthen, toffed his head with an air of confcious fuperiority, and every now and then caft a look of contempt upon his humble companion. In paffing through a wood, they were met by a gang of highwaymen, who im-mediately feized upon the Horfe that was carry-

ing

ing the treafure: but the fpirited fteed, not being altogether difpofed to ftand fo quietly as was neceffary for their purpofe, they beat him moft unmecifully; and after plundering him of his boafted load, left him to lament at his leifure the cruel bruifes he had received. Friend, faid his defpifed companion to him, who had now reafon to triumph in his turn, diftinguifhed pofts are often dangerous to thofe who poffefs them: if you had *ferved a miller*, as I do, you might have travelled the road *unmolefted*

FABLE XLIV.

The Dove and the Ant.

WE fhould be always ready to do good offices, even to the meaneft of our fellow creatures; as there is no one to whofe affiftance we may not, upon fome occafion or other, be greatly indebted.

A Dove was fipping from the banks of a rivulet, when an Ant, who was at the fame time trailing a grain of corn along the edge of the brook, inadvertently fell in. The Dove obferving the helplefs infect ftruggling in vain to reach the fhore, was touched with compaffion; and plucking a blade of grafs, dropped it into the ftream; by

means

means of which the poor Ant, like a ship-wreck-
ed sailor upon a plank, got safe to land. She
had scarcely arrived there, when she perceived a
fowler just going to discharge his piece at her deliverer: upon which she instantly crept up his
foot and stung him on the ankle. The sportsman
starting, occasioned a rustling among the boughs,
which alarmed the Dove, who immediately sprung
up, and by that means escaped the danger with
which she was threatened.

FABLE XLV.

The Parrot.

A Certain Widower, in order to amuse his so-
litary hours, and in some measure supply
the conversation of his departed helpmate of loquacious memory, determined to purchase a Parrot. With this view he applied to a dealer in
birds, who shewed him a large collection of Par-
rots of various kinds. Whilst they were exer-
cising their talkative talents before him, one re-
peating the cries of the town, another asking for
a cup of sack, and a third bawling out for a coach,
he observed a green Parrot, perched in a thought-
ful manner at a distance upon the foot of a table:
And so you, my grave gentleman, said he, are
quite silent. To which the Parrot replied, like

37. Lion, Bear, and Fox.

38. Owl and Nightingale.

39. Ant and Caterpillar.

40. The two Foxes.

41. The conceited Owl.

42. The Fox and Cat.

43. The two Mice.

44. The Dove and the Ant.

45. The Parrot.

46. The Cat and the Bat.

47. The two Lizards.

48. Jupiter's Lottery.

a philofophical bird, "I think the more." Pleafed
with this fenfible anfwer, our Widower immediately paid down his price, and took home the
bird; conceiving great things from a creature,
who had given fo ftriking a fpecimen of his parts.
But after having inftructed him during a whole
month, he found to his great difappointment,
that he could get nothing more from him than
the fatiguing repetition of the fame dull fentence,
" I think the more."   I find, faid he in great
wrath, that thou art a moft invincible fool: and
ten times more a fool was I, for having formed
a favourable opinion of thy abilities upon no
better foundation, than an *affected folemnity.*

F A B L E   XLVI.

The Cat and the Bat.

A Cat having devoured her mafter's favourite
bullfinch, over-heard him threatning to put
her to death the moment he could find her.   In
this diftrefs fhe preferred a prayer to Jupiter;
vowing, if he would deliver her from her prefent
danger, that never while fhe lived would fhe eat
another bird.   Not long afterwards a bat moft
invitingly flew into the room where Pufs was
purring in the window. The queftion was, how
to act upon fo tempting an occafion? Her appe-

tite

tite preffed hard on one fide; and her vow threw fome fcruples in her way on the other. At length fhe hit upon a moft convenient diftinction to remove all difficulties, by determining that as a *bird* indeed it was unlawful prize, but as a *moufe* fhe might very confcientioufly eat it; and accordingly without further debate fell to the repaft.

Thus it is that men are apt to *impofe* upon themfelves by vain and groundlefs diftinctions, when *confcience* and *principle* are at variance with *intereft* and *inclination*.

F A B L E   XLVII.

The two Lizards.

AS two Lizards were bafking under a fouth wall, How contemptible, faid one of them, is our condition! We exift, 'tis true, but that is all: for we hold no fort of rank in the creation, and are utterly unnoticed by the world. Curfed obfcurity! Why was I not rather born a ftag, to range at large, the pride and glory of fome royal foreft? It happened that in the midft of thefe unjuft murmurs, a pack of hounds was heard in full cry after the very creature he was envying, who being quite fpent with the chace, was torn in pieces by the dogs in fight of our two Lizards.

And

And is this the lordly ftag, whofe place in the creation you wifhed to hold? faid the wifer Lizard to his complaining friend: Let his fad fate teach you to blefs providence for placing you in that *humble fituation*, which fecures you from the dangers of a more *elevated rank*.

FABLE XLVIII.

Jupiter's Lottery.

JUPITER, in order to pleafe mankind, directed Mercury to give notice that he had eftablifhed a Lottery, in which there were no blanks: and that, amongft a variety of other valuable chances, Wifdom was the higheft prize. It was Jupiter's command, that in this Lottery, fome of the gods fhould alfo become adventurers. The tickets being difpofed of, and the wheels placed. Mercury was employed to prefide at the drawing. It happened that the beft prize fell to Minerva: upon which a general murmur ran thro' the affembly, and hints were thrown out, that Jupiter had ufed fome unfair practices to fecure this defirable lot to his daughter. Jupiter, that he might at once both *punifh* and *filence* thefe impious clamours of the human race, prefented them with *Folly* in the place of *Wifdom;* with which they went away perfectly well contented:

and

and from that time the *greatest Fools* have always looked upon themselves as the *Wisest Men.*

FABLE XLIX.

The litigious Cats.

TWO Cats having stolen some cheese, could not agree about dividing the prize. In order therefore to settle the dispute, they consented to refer the matter to a Monkey. The proposed arbitrator very readily accepted the office, and producing a ballance, put a part into each scale. "Let me see—(said he) ay—this lump outweighs the other:" and immediately bit off a considerable piece in order to reduce it, he observed, to an equilibrium. The opposite scale was now become the heaviest; which afforded our conscientious judge an additional reason for a second mouthful. Hold, hold, said the two Cats, who began to be alarmed for the event,—give us our respective shares and we are satisfied. If *you* are satisfied, returned the Monkey, *justice* is not: a cause of this intricate nature is by no means *so soon* determined. Upon which he continued to nibble first one piece and then the other, till the poor Cats seeing their cheese gradually diminishing, intreated him to give himself no farther trouble, but deliver to them what remained. Not so fast,

I

I befeech ye friends, replied the Monkey; we owe juftice to ourfelves as well as to you: what remains is due to me in right of my office. Upon which, he crammed the whole into his mouth, and with great gravity difmiffed the court.

FABLE L.

The two Dogs.

HASTY and inconfiderate connexions are generally attended with great difadvantages: and much of every man's good or ill fortune depends upon the *choice* he makes of his *friends.*

A good-natured Spaniel overtook a furly Maftiff, as he was travelling upon the high road. Tray, although an entire ftranger to Tyger, very civily accofted him: And if it would be no interruption, he faid, he fhould be glad to bear him company on his way. Tyger, who happened not to be altogether in fo growling a mood as ufual, accepted the propofal: and they very amicably purfued their journey together. In the midft of their converfation, they arrived at the next village; where Tyger began to difplay his malignant difpofition, by an unprovoked attack upon every dog he met. The villagers immedi-

ately

ately fallied forth with great indignation to refcue their refpective favourites; and falling upon our two friends, without diftinction or mercy, poor Tray was moft cruelly treated, for no other reafon, but his being *found in bad company.*

FABLE LI.

Death and Cupid.

JUPITER fent forth Death and Cupid to travel round the world, giving each of them a bow in his hand, and a quiver of arrows at his back. It was ordered by the fupreme difpofer of all events, that the arrows of *Love* fhould only wound the young, in order to fupply the decays of mortal men; and thofe of *Death* were to ftrike old age, and free the world of an ufelefs charge. Our travellers, being one day extremely fatigued with their journey, refted themfelves under the covert of a wood, and throwing down their arrows in a promifcuous manner before them, they both fell faft afleep. They had not repofed themfelves long, before they were awakened by a fudden noife; when haftily gathering up their arms, each in the confufion took by miftake fome of the darts that belonged to the other. By this means, it frequently happened that *Death* vanquifhed the *young*, and *Cupid* fubdued the *old*.

Jupiter

Jupiter obferved the error, but did not think proper to redrefs it; forefeeing that fome good might arife from their unlucky exchange. And in fact, if men were wife, they would learn from this miftake to be apprehenfive of *death* in their *youth*, and to guard againft the *amorous paffions* in their *old age.*

FABLE LII.

The Mock-bird.

THERE is a certain Bird in the Weft-Indies, which has the faculty of mimicking the notes of every other fongfter, without being able himfelf to add any original ftrains to the concert. As one of thefe Mock-birds was difplaying his talents of ridicule among the branches of a venerable wood: 'Tis very well, faid a little warbler, fpeaking in the name of all the reft, we grant you that *our* mufic is not without its faults: but why will you not favour us with a ftrain of *your own?*

FABLE LIII.

The Spectacles.

HOW strangely all mankind differ in their opinions! and how strongly each is attached to his own!

Jupiter, one day, enjoying himself over a bowl of nectar, and in a merry humour, determined to make mankind a present. Momus was appointed to convey it to them; who mounted on a rapid car, was presently on earth. Come hither, says he, ye happy mortals; great Jupiter has opened for your benefit his all-gracious hands. 'Tis true, he made you somewhat short-sighted, but to remedy that inconvenience, behold, how he has favoured you! So saying, he unloosed his portmanteau; when an infinite number of Spectacles tumbled out, and were picked up by the crowd with all the eagerness imaginable. There was enow for all, every man had his pair. But it was soon found that these Spectacles did not represent objects to all mankind alike: for one pair was *purple*, another *blue*; one was *white*, and another *black:* some of the glasses were *red*, some *green*, and some *yellow*. In short, there were of all manner of colours, and

every

every shade of colour. However, notwithstand-
ing this diversity, every man was charmed with
his own, as believing it the best; and enjoyed
in *opinion*, all the satisfaction of *truth*.

FABLES.

BOOK III.

NEWLY INVENTED.

I 4

FABLE I.

The Red-breast and Sparrow.

AS a Red-breast was singing on a tree by the
side of a rural cottage, a Sparrow perched
upon the thatch took occasion thus to re-
primand him.   And dost *thou*, said he, with thy
dull autumnal note presume to emulate the *Birds
of Spring?* Can *thy* weak warblings pretend to vie
with the sprightly accent of the Thrush and the
Blackbird? with the various melody of the Lark
or Nightingale? Whom other birds, far *thy* superiors. have been long content to admire in silence.
Judge with *candour* at least, replied the Robin;
nor impute those efforts to *ambition* solely, which

may

may *sometimes* flow from *Love of the Art.* I reverence indeed, but by no means envy, the birds whose fame has stood the test of ages. Their songs *have* charmed both hill and dale; but their season is past, and their throats are silent. I feel not, however, the ambition to surpass or equal them: my efforts are of a much humbler nature; and I may surely hope for pardon, while I endeavour to chear those forsaken valleys, by an attempt to *imitate the strains I love.*

F A B L E II.

The two Bees.

ON a fine morning in May, two Bees set forward in quest of honey; the one wise and temperate, the other careless and extravagant. They soon arrived at a garden enriched with aromatic herbs; the most fragrant flowers, and the most delicious fruits. They regaled themselves for a time on the various dainties that were spread before them: the one loading his thigh at intervals with provisions for the hive against the distant winter; the other, revelling in sweets without regard to any thing but his present gratification. At length they found a wide-mouthed phial, that hung beneath the bough of a peach-tree, filled with honey ready tempered, and exposed

posed

posed to their taste in the most alluring manner. The thoughtless *Epicure*, spite of all his friend's remonstrances, plunged headlong into the vessel, resolving to indulge himself in all the pleasures of sensuality. The *Philosopher*, on the other hand, sipped a little with caution, but being suspicious of danger, flew off to fruits and flowers; where by the moderation of his meals, he improved his relish for the true enjoyment of them. In the evening, however, he called upon his friend, to enquire whether he would return to the hive; but found him surfeited in sweets, which he was as unable to *leave*, as to *enjoy*. Clogged in his wings, enfeebled in his feet, and his whole frame totally enervated, he was but just able to bid his friend adieu, and to lament with his latest breath, that though a taste of pleasure might quicken the relish of life, an unrestrained indulgence is inevitable destruction.

FABLE III.

The Diamond and the Glow-worm.

A Diamond happened to fall from the *solitaire* of a young lady, as she was walking one evening on a terrace in the garden. A Glow-worm who had beheld it sparkling in its descent, soon as the gloom of night had eclipsed its lustre,

began

began to mock and to infult it. Art thou that wonderous thing, that vaunteft of fuch prodigious brightnefs? Where now is all thy boafted brilliancy? Alas, in evil hour has fortune thrown thee within the reach of my fuperior blaze. Conceited infect, replied the Gem, thou oweft thy feeble glimmer to the darknefs that furrounds thee: know, my luftre bears the teft of day, and even derives its chief advantage from that diftinguifhing light, which difcovers thee to be no more than a dark and paltry Worm.

FABLE IV.

The Oftrich and the Pelican.

THE Oftrich one day met the Pelican, and obferving her breaft all bloody, Good God! fays fhe to her, what is the matter? What accident has befallen you? You certainly have been feized by fome favage beaft of prey, and have with difficulty efcaped from his mercilefs claws. Do not be furprifed, friend, replied the Pelican: no fuch accident, nor indeed, any thing more than common, hath happened to me. I have only been engaged in my ordinary employment of tending my neft, of feeding my dear little ones, and nourifhing them with the vital blood from my bofom. Your anfwer, returned the Of-

trich,

49 The litigious
Cats.

50 The two
Dogs.

51 Death disguised.

52 The
Mock-bird.

53 The
Spectacles.

trich, astonishes me still more than the horrid figure you make. What! is this your practice, to tear your own flesh, to spill your own blood, and to sacrifice yourself in this cruel manner to the important cravings of your young ones? I know not which to pity most, your misery, or your folly. Be advised by me; have some regard for yourself; and leave off this barbarous custom of mangling your own body: as for your children, commit them to the care of providence, and make yourself quite easy about them. My example may be of use to you. I lay my eggs upon the ground, and just cover them lightly over with sand: if they have the good luck to escape being crushed by the tread of man or beast, the warmth of the sun broods upon, and hatches them: and in due time my young ones come forth: I leave them to be nursed by nature, and fostered by the elements; I give myself no trouble about them, and I neither know nor care what becomes of them. Unhappy wretch, says the Pelican, who art hardened against thy offspring, and through want of natural affection renderest thy travail fruitless to thyself! who knowest not the sweets of a parent's anxiety, the tender delight of a mother's sufferings! It is not I, but thou that art cruel to thy own flesh. Thy insensibility may exempt thee from a tem-

porary

porary inconvenience, and an inconfiderable pain; but at the fame time it makes thee inattentive to a moſt neceſſary duty, and incapable of reliſhing the pleaſure that attends it: a pleaſure, the moſt exquifite that nature hath indulged to us; in which pain itſelf is ſwallowed up and loſt, or only ſerves to heighten the enjoyment.

FABLE V.

The Hounds in Couples.

A Huntſman was leading forth his Hounds one morning to the chafe, and had linked feveral of the young Dogs in Couples, to prevent their following every fcent, and hunting diforderly, as their own inclinations and fancy ſhould direct them. Among others, it was the fate of Jowler and Vixen to be thus yoked together. Jowler and Vixen were both young and unexperienced; but had for fome time been conſtant companions, and feemed to have entertained a great fondnefs for each other; they uſed to be perpetually playing together, and in any quarrel that happened, always took one another's part; it might have been expected therefore, that it would not be difagreeable to them to be ſtill more clofely united. However in fact it proved otherwife: they had not been long joined toge-

ther

ther before both parties were obferved to exprefs uneafinefs at their prefent fituation. Different inclinations and oppofite wills began to difcover and to exert themfelves: if one chofe to go this way, the other was as eager to take the contrary; if one was preffing forward, the other was fure to lag behind; Vixen pulled back Jowler, and Jowler dragged along Vixen, Jowler growled at Vixen, and Vixen fnapped at Jowler: till at laft it came to a downright quarrel between them; and Jowler treated Vixen in a very rough and ungenerous manner, without any regard to the inferiority of her ftrength, or the tendernefs of her fex. As they were thus continually vexing and tormenting one another, an old Hound, who had obferved all that paffed, came up to them, and thus reproved them: "What a couple of filly Puppies you are, to be perpetually worrying yourfelves at this rate! What hinders your going on peaceably and quietly together? Cannot you compromife the matter between you, by each confulting the other's inclination a little! at leaft, try to make a virtue of neceffity, and fubmit to what you cannot remedy: you cannot get rid of the chains; but you may make them fit eafy upon you. I am an old Dog, and let my age and experience inftruct you: when I was in the fame circumftance with you, I foon found.

that

that thwarting my companion, was only tormenting myfelf; and my yoke-fellow happily came into the fame way of thinking. We endeavoured
to join in the fame purfuits, and to follow one
another's inclinations; and fo we jogged on together, not only with eafe and quiet, but with
comfort and pleafure. We found by experience,
that mutual compliance not only compenfates for
liberty, but is even attended with a fatisfaction
and delight, beyond what liberty itfelf can give."

FABLE VI.

The Mifer and the Magpye.

AS a Mifer fate at his defk, counting over his
heaps of gold; a Magpye eloping from his
cage, picked up a guinea, and hopped away
with it. The Mifer, who never failed to count
his money over a fecond time, immediately
miffed the piece, and rifing up from his feat in
the utmoft confternation, obferved the felon
hiding it in a crevice of the floor. And art *thou*,
cried he, that worft of thieves, *who* haft robbed
me of my gold, without the plea of neceffity,
and without regard to its proper ufe? But thy
life fhall attone for fo prepofterous a villany.
Soft words, good mafter, quoth the Magpy.
Have I then injured you, in any other fenfe
than

than you defraud the public? And am I *not using* your money in the fame manner you do your-felf? If I muft lofe my life for hiding a fingle guinea, what do you, I pray, deferve, who fe-crete fo many thoufands?

FABLE VII.

The Senfitive Plant and the Thiftle.

A Thiftle happened to fpring up very near to a Senfitive Plant. The former obferving the extreme bafhfulnefs and delicacy of the lat-ter, addreffed her in the following manner. Why are you fo modeft and referved, my good neighbour, as to withdraw your leaves at the approach of ftrangers? Why do you fhrink as if you were afraid. from the touch of every hand? Take example and advice from me: if I liked not their familiarity, I would make them keep their diftance. nor fhould any fawcy finger pro-voke me unrevenged. Our tempers and quali-ties, replied the other, are widely different. I have neither the ability nor inclination to give offence: you it feems are by no means deftitute of either. My defire is to live peaceably in the ftation wherein I am placed; and though my humility may now and then caufe me a moment's uneafinefs, it tends on the whole to preferve my
tranquility.

K

tranquility. The cafe is otherwife with you, whofe irritable temper, amd revengeful difpofition, will probably one time or other be the caufe of your deftruction. While they were thus arguing the point, the gardiner came with his little fpaddle, in order to lighten the earth round the ftem of the Senfitive Plant; but perceiving the Thiftle, he thruft his inftrument thro' the root of it, and directly toffed it out of his garden.

FABLE VIII.

The Poet and the Death-watch.

AS a Poet fate in his clofet, feafting his imagination on the hopes of fame and immortality; he was ftartled on a fudden with the ominous found of a Death-watch. However, immediately recollecting himfelf—Vain infect, faid he. ceafe thy impertinent forebodings, fufficient indeed to frighten the weaknefs of women or of children: but far beneath the notice of a Poet and a Philofopher. As for me, whatever accident may threaten my life; my fame, fpite of thy prognoftics, fhall live to future ages. May be fo, replied the infect, I find at leaft, thou had'ft rather liften to the Moggot in thy head, than to the Worm beneath thy table; but know,

that

that the fuggeſtions of vanity are altogether as deceitful as thoſe of ſuperſtition.

FABLE IX.

Pythagoras and the Critic.

PYTHAGORAS was one day very earneſtly engaged in taking an exact meaſure of the length of the olympic courſe. One of thoſe conceited Critics, who aim at every thing, and are ready to interpoſe with their opinion upon all ſubjects, happened to be preſent; and could not help ſmiling to himſelf to ſee the Philoſopher ſo employed, and to obſerve what great attention and pains he beſtowed upon ſuch a buſineſs. And pray, ſays he, accoſting Pythagoras, may I preſume to aſk, with what deſign you have given yourſelf this trouble? Of that, replied the Philoſopher; I ſhall very readily inform you. We are aſſured, that Hercules when he inſtituted the olympic games, himſelf laid out this courſe by meaſure, and determined it to the length of ſix hundred feet, meaſuring it by the ſtandard of his own foot. Now by taking an exact meaſure of this ſpace, and ſeeing how much it exceeds the meaſure of the ſame number of feet now in uſe, we can find how much the foot of Hercules, and in proportion his whole

K 2

ſtature,

ſtature, exceeded that of the preſent generation. A very curious ſpeculation truly, ſays the Critic, and of great uſe and importance, no doubt! And ſo you will demonſtrate to us, that the bulk of this fabulous hero was equal to his extravagant enterpriſes and his marvellous exploits. And pray Sir, what may be the reſult of your enquiry at laſt? I ſuppoſe, you can now tell me exactly to a hair's breadth, how tall Hercules was. The reſult of my enquiry, replied the Philoſopher, is this; and it is a concluſion of greater uſe and importance, than you ſeem to expect from it; that if you will always eſtimate the labours of the philoſopher, the deſigns of the patriot, and the actions of the hero, by the ſtandard of your own narrow conceptions, you will ever be greatly miſtaken in your judgment concerning them.

FABLE X.

The Bear.

A Bear who was bred in the ſavage deſarts of *Siberia*, had an inclination to ſee the world. He travelled from foreſt to foreſt, and from one kingdom to another, making many profound obſervations in his way. Among the reſt of his excurtions, he came by accident into a farmer's yard, where he ſaw a number of poultry ſtand-

ing

1 The Redbreast & the Sparrow.
2 The two Bees.
3 The Diamond and ye Glow-worm.
4 The Ostrich and ye Pelican.
5 the Hounds in couples.
6 The Miser & the Magpye.
7 The Sensitive Plant & Thistle.
8 the Poet & the Death watch.
9 Pythagoras and the Critic.
10 The Bear.
11 The Stork & the Crow.
12 Echo and the Owl.

ing to drink by the side of a pool. Observing
that after every sip they turned up their heads
toward the sky, he could not forbear enquiring
the reason of so peculiar a ceremony. They told
him, that it was by way of returning thanks to
heaven for the benefits they received; and was
indeed an ancient and religious custom, which
they could not, with a safe conscience, or without impiety, omit. Here the Bear burst into a
fit of laughter, at once mimicking their gestures,
and ridiculing their superstition, in the most
contemptuous manner. On this, the Cock,
with a spirit suitable to the boldness of his character, addressed him in the following words.
As you are a stranger, Sir, you perhaps may be
excused the indecency of this behaviour; yet
give me leave to tell you, that none but a *Bear*
would ridicule any religious ceremonies whatso-
ever, in the presence of those who believe them
of importance.

F A B L E XI.

The Stork and the Crow.

A Stork and a Crow had once a strong contention, which of them stood highest in the
favour of Jupiter. The Crow alledged his skill
in omens, his infallibility in prophecies, and
K 3

his

his great ufe to the priefts of that deity in all their facrifices and religious ceremonies. The Stork urged only his blamelefs life, the care he took to preferve his offspring, and the affiftance he lent his parents under the infirmities of age. It happened, as it generally does in religious difputes, that neither of them could confute the other; fo they both agreed to refer the decifion to Jupiter himfelf. On their joint application, the god determined thus between them. Let *none* of my creatures defpair of my regard: I know their weaknefs; I pity their errors; and whatever is well meant, I accept as it was intended. Yet facrifices or ceremonies are in *themfelves* of no importance, and every attempt to penetrate the counfels of the gods, is altogether as vain as it is prefumptuous: but he who pays to Jupiter a juft honour and reverence, who leads the moft temperate life, and who does the moft good in proportion to his abilities; as he beft anfwers the end of his creation, will affuredly ftand higheft in the favour of his creator.

FABLE

F A B L E XII.

Echo and the Owl.

THE vain hear the flatteries of their own imagination, and fancy them to be the voice
of fame.

A folemn Owl puffed up with vanity, fate re-
peating her *fcreams* at midnight, from the hollow
of a blafted oak. And whence, cryed fhe, proceeds this awful filence, unlefs it be to favour my
fuperior melody? Surely the groves are hufht
in expectation of my voice, and when I fing, all
nature liftens. An Echo refounding from an
adjacent rock, replied immediately, "all nature
liftens." The nightingale, refumed fhe, has
ufurped the fovereignty by night: *her* note indeed
is mufical, but mine is fweeter far. The voice
confirming her opinion, replied again, "is
fweeter far." Why then am I diffident, continued fhe, why do I fear to join the tuneful
choir? The Echo ftill flattering her vanity repeated, "join the tuneful choir." Roufed by this
empty phantom of encouragement, fhe on the
morrow mingled her hootings with the harmony
of the groves. But the tuneful fongfters, difgufted with her noife, and affronted by her im-

K 4   pudence,

pudence, unanimoufly drove her from their fociety, and ftill continue to purfue her wherever fhe appears.

FABLE XIII.

Prometheus.

PROMETHEUS formed man of the fineft clay, and animated his work with fire ftolen from heaven. He endowed him with all the faculties that are to be found amongft the animal creation: he gave him the courage of the lion, the fubtlety of the fox, the providence of the ant, and the induftry of the bee; and he enabled him, by the fuperiority of his underftanding, to fubdue them all, and to make them fubfervient to his ufe and pleafure. He difcovered to him the metals hidden in the bowels of the earth, and fhewed him their feveral ufes. He inftructed him in every thing that might tend to cultivate and civilize human life: he taught him to till the ground, and to improve the fertility of nature; to build houfes, to cover himfelf with garments, and to defend himfelf againft the inclemencies of the air and the feafons; to compound medicines of falutary herbs, to heal wounds, and to cure difeafes; to conftruct fhips, to crofs the feas, and to communicate to every

country

country the riches of all. In a word, he indued him with fenfe and memory, with fagacity and invention, with art and fcience: and to crown all, he gave him an infight into futurity. But, alas! this latter gift, inftead of improving, wholly deftroyed the proper effect of all the former. Furnifhed with all the means and inftruments of happinefs, man neverthelefs was miferable; through the knowledge and dread of future evil, he was incapable of enjoying prefent good. Prometheus faw, and immediately refolved to remedy this inconvenience: he effectually reftored man to a capacity of happinefs, by depriving him of *prefcience*, and giving him *hope* in its ftead.

F A B L E XIV.

Momus.

'TIS faid that Momus was perpetually blaming and ridiculing whatever he faw. Even the works of the gods themfelves could not efcape his univerfal cenfure. The eyes of the bull, he faid, were fo placed by Jupiter, that they could not direct his horns in pufhing at his enemies. The houfes which Minerva had inftructed men to build, were contrived fo very injudicioufly, that they could not be removed from a bad neighbourhood, nor from any other inconvenience.

In

In short, the frame of man himself was in *his* opinion extremely defective; having no window in his bofom, that might demonſtrate his ſincerity. or betray his wicked purpoſes and prevent their execution. Theſe and many other faults were found in the productions of nature; but when he ſurveyed the works of art, there was no end of his altercation. Jupiter, being reſolved to try how far his malice would proceed, ſent his daughter Venus to deſire that he would give his opinion of her beauty. She appeared accordingly before the churliſh god, trembling at the apprehenſion of his known ſeverity. He examined her proportions with all the rigour of an envious critic. But her ſhape and complexion were ſo ſtriking, and her ſmiles and graces ſo very engaging, that he found it impoſſible to give the leaſt colour to any objection he could make. Yet, to ſhew how hard malevolence will ſtruggle for a cavil; as ſhe was retiring from his preſence, he begged ſhe would acquaint her father, that whatever graces might be in her motion, yet—*her ſlippers were too noiſy.*

F A B L E.

FABLE XV.

The Butterfly, the Snail, and the Bee.

A Butterfly proudly perched on the gawdy leaves of a French marygold, was boasting the vast extent and variety of his travels. I have ranged, said he, over the graceful and majestic scenes of * *Hagley*, and have feasted my eyes with elegance and variety at † *The Leasowes*. I have wandered through regions of Eglantine and Honey-suckle, I have revelled in kisses on beds of Violets and cowslips, and have enjoyed the delicious fragrance of Roses and Carnations. In short, my fancy unbounded, and my flights unrestrained, I have visited with perfect freedom all the flowers of the field or garden, and must be allowed to *know the world*, in a superlative degree.

A Snail, who hung attentive to his wonders on a cabbage-leaf, was struck with admiration; and concluded him, from all this experience, to be the wisest of animal creation.

It happened that a Bee pursued her occupation on a neighbouring bed of marjoram, and having

heard

* *Lord Lyttelton's.*   † *Mr. Shenstone's.*

heard our oftentatious vagrant, reprimanded him in this manner. Vain, empty flutterer, faid fhe, whom inftruction cannot improve, nor experience itfelf enlighten! Thou haft rambled over the world; wherein does thy knowledge of it confift? Thou haft feen variety of objects; what conclufions haft thou drawn from them? Thou haft tafted of every amufement; haft thou extracted any thing for *ufe?* I too am a traveller: go and look into my hive; and let my treafures *intimate* to thee, that the end of travelling is, to collect materials either for the ufe and emolument of *private life,* or for the advantage of the *community.*

F A B L E XVI.

The Tuberofe and the Sun-flower.

A Tuberofe in a bow-window on the north-fide of a ftately villa, addreffed a Sun-flower which grew on a flope, that was contiguous to the houfe. Pray, fays he, neighbour *Turnfole,* to what purpofe do you pay all this devotion to that fictitious deity of yours, the Sun? Why are you continually diftorting your body, and cafting up your eyes to that glaring luminary? What fuperftition induces you to think, that we flowers exift only through *his* influence? Both

you

you and I are furely indebted to the hot-bed, and
to the diligence of the gardiner, for our production and fupport.   For *my* part, I fhall referve
my homage, together with my fweets, for that
benevolent mafter who is continually watering
and refrefhing me: nor do I defire ever to fee
the face of that Sun you fo vainly idolize, while
I can enjoy the cool fhade of this magnificent fa-
loon.   Truce with thy blafphemics, replied the
Sun-flower: why doft thou revile that glorious
being, who difpenfes life and vigour, not only
to *us*, but to every part of the creation? Without this, alas! how ineffectual were the fkill and
vigilance of thy boafted mafter, either to fupport *thy* tender frame, or even to preferve his
own! But this muft ever be the cafe with fuch
contracted underftandings: fufficient, indeed, to
point out our more immediate benefactors, without regarding the original fource, from which
all beneficence proceeds.

F A B L E XVII.

The Magpye and the Raven.

THERE was a certain Magpye, more bufy
and more loquacious than any of his tribe.
His tongue was in perpetual motion, and himfelf continually upon the wing; fluttering from

place

place to place, and very feldom appearing twice together in the fame company.

Sometimes you faw him with a flock of pigeons, plundering a field of new fown corn; anon, perched upon a cherry-tree with a parcel of tom-tits: the next moment, you would be furprifed to find the fame individual bird engaged with a flight of crows, and feafting upon a carcafe.

He took it one day into his head to vifit an old Raven who lived retired among the branches of a venerable oak; and there, at the foot of a lonely mountain, had paffed near half a century.

I admire, faid the prating bird, your moft romantic fituation, and the wildnefs of thefe rocks and precipices around you: I am abfolutely tranfported with the murmur of that water-fall: methinks it diffufes a tranquility, furpaffing all the joys of publick life. What an agreeable fequeftration from worldly buftle and impertinence! what an opportunity of contemplating the divine beauties of nature! I fhall moft certainly, quit the gaieties of town, and for the fake of thefe rural fcenes, and my good friend's converfation, pafs the remainder of my days in the folitude he has chofen.

Well,

Well, Sir, replies the Raven, I shall be at all times glad to receive you in my old-fashioned way; but *you* and *I* should certainly prove most unsuitable companions. *Your* whole ambition is to shine in company, and to recommend yourself to the world by univerfal complaifance; whereas *my* greateft happinefs confifts in eafe and privacy, and the felect converfation of a few whom I efteem. I prefer a good heart to the moft voluble tongue; and tho' much obliged to you for the politenefs of your profeffions, yet I fee your benevolence divided among fo *nume-rous* an *acquaintance,* that a very flender fhare of it can remain for thofe you are pleafed to honour with the name of *friend.*

F A B L E XVIII.

The Diamond and the Loadstone.

A Diamond of great beauty and luftre, obferving, not only many other gems of a lower clafs ranged together with him in the fame cabinet, but a Loadftone likewife placed not far from him; began to queftion the latter how he came there; and what pretenfions he had to be ranked among the precious ftones: he, who appeared to be no better than a mere flint; a forry, coarfe, rufty-looking pebble; without any the

leaft

leaſt ſhining quality to advance him to ſuch an honour: and concluded with deſiring him to keep his diſtance, and pay a proper reſpect to his ſuperiors. I find, ſaid the Loadſtone, you judge by external appearances; and it is your intereſt, that others ſhould form their judgment by the ſame rule. I muſt own I have nothing to boaſt of in that reſpect; but I may venture to ſay, that I make amends for my outward defects, by my inward qualities. The great improvement of navigation in theſe latter ages is intirely owing to me. It is owing to me, that the diſtant parts of the world are known and acceſſible to each other; that the remoteſt nations are connected together, and all in a manner united into one common ſociety; that by a mutual intercourſe they relieve one another's wants, and all enjoy the ſeveral bleſſings peculiar to each. Great Britain is indebted to me for her wealth, her ſplendour, and her power; and the arts and ſciences are in a great meaſure obliged to me for their late improvements, and their continual in-creaſe. I am willing to allow you your due praiſe in its full extent; you are a very pretty bawble; I am mightily delighted to ſee you glitter and ſparkle; I look upon you with plea-ſure and ſurpriſe: but I muſt be convinced that you are of ſome ſort of uſe, before I acknow-

ledge

ledge that you have any real merit, or treat you with that refpect which you feem to demand.

F A B L E XIX.

The Boy and the Nettle.

A Little Boy playing in the fields, chanced to be ftung by a Nettle, and came crying to his father: he told him, he had been hurt by that nafty weed feveral times before; that he was always afraid of it: and that now he did but juft touch it, as lightly as poffible, when he was fo feverely ftung. Child, faid he, your touching it fo gently and timoroufly is the very *reafon* of its hurting you. A Nettle may be handled fafely, if you do it with courage and refolution: if you feize it boldly, and gripe it faft, be affured it will never fting you; and you will meet with many forts of *perfons*, as well as *things* in the world, which ought to be treated in the very fame manner.

F A B L E XX.

The Monfter in the Sun.

AN Aftronomer was obferving the Sun thro' a Telefcope, in order to take an exact draught of the feveral fpots, which appear upon the face

L

of

of it. While he was intent upon his obferva-
tions, he was on a fudden furprifed with a new
and aftonifhing appearance; a large portion of
the furface of the Sun was at once covered by a
Monfter of enormous fize, and horrible form; it
had an immenfe pair of wings, a great number
of legs, and a long and vaft probofcis; and that
it was alive, was very apparent, from its quick
and violent motions, which the obferver could,
from time to time, plainly perceive. Being fure
of the fact, (for how could he be miftaken in
what he faw fo clearly?) our Philofopher began
to draw many furprifing conclufions from pre-
mifes fo well eftablifhed. He calculated the magnitude of this extraordinary animal; and found
that he covered about two fquare degrees of the
Sun's furface; that placed upon the earth he
would fpread over half one hemefphere of it; and
that he was feven or eight times as big as the
moon. But what was moft aftonifhing, was the
prodigious heat that he muft endure: it was
plain that he was fomething of the nature of the
falamander, but of a far more fiery temperament;
for it was demoftrable from the cleareft princi-
ples, that in his prefent fituation he muft have
acquired a degree of heat two thoufand times ex-
ceeding that of red-hot iron. It was a Problem
worth confidering, whether he fubfifted upon

the

the grofs vapours of the Sun, and fo from time
to time cleared away thofe fpots which they are
perpetually forming, and which would otherwife
wholly obfcure and incruftate its face; or whether
it might not feed on the folid fubftance of the
orb itfelf, which by this means, together with
the conftant expence of light, muft foon be exhaufted and confumed; or whether he was not
now and then fupplied by the falling of fome
eccentric Comet into the Sun. However this
might be, he found by computation, that the
earth would be but fhort allowance for him for
a few months: and farther, it was no improbable conjecture, that as the earth was deftined to
be deftroyed by fire, this fiery flying Monfter
would remove hither at the appointed time, and
might much more eafily and conveniently effect
a conflagration, than any other Comet, hitherto provided for that fervice. In the earneft purfuit of thefe, and many the like deep and curious fpeculations, the Aftronomer was engaged,
and was preparing to communicate them to the
public. In the mean time, the difcovery began
to be much talked of; all the *virtuofi* gathered together to fee fo ftrange a fight. They were equally
convinced of the accuracy of the obfervation, and
of the conclufions fo clearly deduced from it. At
laft, one, more cautious than the reft, was re-

L 2

folved,

folved, before he gave a full affent to the report of his fenfes, to examine the whole procefs of the affair, and all the parts of the inftrument: he opened the Telefcope, and behold! a fmall Fly was inclofed in it, which having fettled on the center of the object-glafs, had given occafion to all this marvellous Theory.

How often do men, thro' prejudice and paffion, thro' envy and malice, fix upon the brighteft and moft exalted characters, the groffeft and moft improbable imputations. It behoves us upon fuch occafions to be upon our guard, and to fufpend our judgments; the fault perhaps is not in the *object,* but in the *mind* of the obferver.

F A B L E XXI.

The difcontented Bee.

A Bee complained to Jupiter, of the numerous evils to which her condition was expofed. Her body, fhe faid, was weak and feeble, yet was fhe condemned to get her living by perpetual toil; fhe was benumbed by the cold of winter, and relaxed by the heat of fummer. Her haunts were infefted with poifonous weeds, and her flights obftructed by ftorms and tempefts. In

fhort,

Plate 148.
13. Prometheus.
14. Momus.
15. The Butterfly, ye Snail & ye Bee.
16. The Icehouse & the Sunflower.
17. the Magpye & the Raven.
18. the Diamond & ye Loadstone.
19. The Boy and the Nettle.
20. the Monster in the Sun.
21. The Discontented Bee.
22. The Snipe Shooter.
23. The Beggar and his Son.
24. The Sun & the Vapour.

fhort, what with dangers from without, and difeafes from within, her life was rendered one continual fcene of anxiety and wretchednefs. Behold
now, faid Jupiter, the frowardnefs and folly of
this unthankful race! The flowers of the field I
have fpread before them as a feaft, and have endeavoured to regale them with an endlefs variety.
They now revel on odoriferous beds of thyme
and lavender, and now on the ftill more fragrant banks of violets and rofes. The bufinefs they
complain of, is the extraction of honey; and, to
alleviate their toil, I have allowed them wings,
which readily tranfport them from one banquet
to another. Storms, tempefts, and noxious
weeds, I have given them fagacity to fhun; and
if ever they are mifled, 'tis thro' the preverfenefs
of their inclinations. But thus it is with *Bees*,
and thus with *Men:* they mifconftrue the benevolence of my defigns, and then complain that
my decrees are rigid: they ungratefully overlook
all the advantages, and magnify all the inconveniences of their ftation. But let my creatures
purfue their happinefs, thro' the paths marked
out by nature; and they will then feel no pains,
which they have not pleafures to compenfate.

L 3

FABLE

FABLE XXII.

The Snipe Shooter.

AS a sportsman ranged the fields with his gun, attended by an experienced old Spaniel, he happened to spring a Snipe; and almost at the same instant, a covey of Partridges. Surprised at the accident, and divided in his aim, he let fly too indeterminately, and by this means missed them *both*. Ah, my good Master, said the Spaniel, you should never have two aims at once. Had you not been dazzled and seduced by the extravagant hope of Partridge, you would most probably have secured your Snipe.

FABLE XXIII.

The Beggar and his Dog.

A Beggar and his Dog sate at the gate of a noble Courtier, and were preparing to make a meal on a bowl of fragments from the Kitchenmaid. A poor Dependant of his Lordship's, who had been sharing the singular favour of a dinner at the steward's table, was struck with their appearance, and stopped a little to observe them. The Beggar, hungry and voracious as any Courtier in Christendom, seized with greediness the

choicest

choiceſt morſels, and ſwallowed them himſelf; the reſidue was divided into portions for his children. A ſcrag was thruſt into one pocket for *honeſt* Jack, a cruſt into another for *baſhful* Tom, and a luncheon of cheeſe was wrapt up with care for the little favourite of his *hopeful* family. In ſhort, if any thing was thrown to the Dog, it was a bone ſo cloſely picked, that it ſcarce afforded a pittance to keep life and ſoul together. How exactly alike, ſaid the Dependant, is this poor Dog's caſe and mine! He is watching for a dinner from a Maſter who cannot ſpare it; I for a place from a needy Lord, whoſe wants perhaps are greater than my own; and whoſe relations, more clamorous than any of this Beggar's brats. Shrewdly was it ſaid by an ingenious writer. a *Courtier's Dependant* is a *Beggar's Dog.*

F A B L E XXIV.

The Sun and the Vapour.

IN the evening of a ſummer's day, as the Sun deſcended behind the weſtern hills, he beheld a thick and unwholeſome Vapour extending itſelf over the whole face of the vallies. Every ſhrub and every flower immediately folded up its leaves, and ſhrunk from the touch of this deteſted *enemy.* Well haſt thou choſen, ſaid the God of day,

                                 this

this the hour of my departure, to spread thy pestilential influence, and taint the beauties of the creation. Enjoy for a short space the notable triumphs of thy malignity. I shall return again with the morning, repair thy mischiefs, and put an end to thy existence. May the *Slanderer* in *thy fate* discern his *own*, and be warned to dread the return of the *Truth*.

FABLE XXV.

Love and Folly.

IN the most early state of things, and among the eldest of beings, existed that God, as the poets entitle him, or rather that Dæmon, as Plato calls him, whose name is Love. He was assisting to the father of the Gods in reducing Chaos into order, in establishing the harmony of the universe, and in regulating and putting in execution the laws, by which the operations of nature are performed, and the frame of the world subsists. Universal good seemed to be his only study, and he was the supreme delight both of Gods and men. But in process of time, among other disorders that arose in the universe, it appeared, that Love began to deviate very often from what had seemed, till now, to be his chief pursuit: he would raise frequent disturbances and confusion

in

in the courfe of nature; though it was always under the pretence of maintaining order and agreement. It feems he had entered into a very intimate acquaintance with a perfon, who had but lately made her appearance in the world. This perfon was Folly, the daughter of Pride and Ignorance. They were often together, and, as often as they were, fome mifchief was fure to be the confequence. By degrees he introduced her into the heavens; where it was their great joy by various artifices to lead the Gods into fuch meafures, as involved them in many inconveniences, and expofed them to much ridicule. They deluded them all in their turns, except Minerva, the only divinity that efcaped their wiles. Even Jupiter himfelf was induced by them to take fome fteps not at all fuitable to the dignity of his character. Folly had gotten the intire afcendant over her companion; however, fhe was refolved to make ftill more fure of him, and engrofs him wholly to herfelf: with this defign fhe infufed a certain intoxicating juice into his nectar, the effects of which were fo powerful, that in the end it utterly deprived him of his fight. Love was too much prejudiced in her favour, to happrehend her to be the caufe of his misfortune; nor indeed did he feem to be in the leaft fenfible of his condition. But his mother

Venus

Venus foon found it out: and in the excefs of her grief and rage carried her complaint to Jupiter, conjuring him to punifh the forcerefs, who had blinded her fon. Jupiter, willing to clear the heavens of fuch troublefome company, called both parties before him, and inquired into their conduct. after a full hearing, he determined, that Folly fhould make fome fort of reparation for the injury done to Love: and being refolved to punifh both for the many irregularities which they had lately introduced, he condemned Love to wander about the earth, and ordered Folly to be his guide.

F A B L E XXVI.

The Eclipfe.

ONE day when the Moon was under an Eclipfe, fhe complained thus to the Sun of the difcontinuance of his favours. My deareft friend, faid fhe, why do you not fhine upon me as you ufed to do? Do I *not* fhine upon thee? faid the Sun; I am very fure that I *intend* it. O no, replies the Moon, but I now perceive the reafon. I fee that dirty planet, the Earth, is got between us.

The

The good influences of the great world would perhaps be more diffusive, were it not for their mischievous dependants, who are so frequently suffered to interpose.

F A B L E   XXVII.

The Boy and the Butterfly.

A Boy, greatly smitten with the colours of a Butterfly, pursued it from flower to flower with indefatigable pains. First he aimed to surprise it among the leaves of a rose; then to cover it with his hat, as it was feeding on a daisy; now hoped to secure it, as it rested on a sprig of myrtle; and now grew sure of his prize, perceiving it loiter on a bed of violets. But the fickle Fly, continually changing one blossom for another, still eluded his attempts. At length, observing it half buried in the cup of a tulip, he rushed forward, and snatching it with violence, crushed it all to pieces. The dying insect, seeing the poor Boy somewhat chagrined at his disappointment, addressed him with all the calmness of a stoic, in the following manner.—Behold, now the end of thy unprofitable sollicitude! and learn, for the benefit of thy future life, that all pleasure is but a painted Butterfly: which, although it may serve to amuse thee in the pur-

suit,

fuit, if embraced with too much ardour, will perish in thy grasp.

FABLE XXVIII.

The Toad and Ephemeron.

AS some workmen were digging marble in a mountain of Scythia, they discerned a Toad of an enormous size in the midst of a solid rock. They were very much surprised at so uncommon an appearance, and the more they considered the circumstances of it, the more their wonder increased. It was hard to conceive by what means this creature had preserved life and received nourishment in so narrow a prison; and still more difficult to account for his birth and existence in a place so totally inaccessible to all of his species. They could conclude no other, than that he was formed together with the rock in which he had been bred, and was coeval with the mountain itself. While they were pursuing these speculations, the Toad sate swelling and bloating, till he was ready to burst with pride and self-importance; to which at last he thus gave vent:——Yes, says he, you behold in me a specimen of the Antediluvian race of animals. I was begotten before the flood; and who is there among the present upstart race of mortals, that

shall

shall dare to contend with me in nobility of birth, or dignity of character? An Ephemeron, sprung that morning from the river Hypanis, as he was flying about from place to place, chanced to be present, and observed all that passed with great attention and curiosity. Vain boaster, says he, what foundation hast thou for pride, either in thy descent, merely because it is ancient, or thy life, because it hath been long? What good qualities hast thou received from thy ancestors? Insignificant even to thyself, as well as useless to others, thou art almost as insensible as the block in which thou wast bred. Even I, that had my birth only from the scum of the neighbouring river, at the rising of this day's sun, and who shall die at its setting, have more reason to applaud my condition, than thou hast to be proud of thine. I have enjoyed the warmth of the sun, the light of the day, and the purity of the air: I have flown from stream to stream, from tree to tree, and from the plain to the mountain: I have provided for posterity, and shall leave behind me a numerous offspring to people the next age of to-morrow: in short, I have fulfilled all the ends of my being, and I have been happy. My whole life, 'tis true, is but of twelve hours: but even one hour of it is to be preferred to a thousand years of mere exiſtence: which have been ſpent, like thine, in ſloth, ignorance, and ſtupidity.

FABLE XXIX.

The Peacock.

THE Peacock, who at firſt was diſtinguiſhed only by a creſt of feathers, preferred a petition to Juno, that he might be honoured alſo with a train. As the bird was a particular favourite, Juno readily enough aſſented; and his train was ordered to ſurpaſs that of every fowl in the creation. The Minion, conſcious of his ſuperb appearance, thought it requiſite to aſſume a proportionable dignity of gait and manners. The common poultry of the farm-yard were quite aſtoniſhed at his magnificence; and even the pheaſants themſelves, beheld him with an eye of envy.—But when he attempted to *fly*, he perceived himſelf to have ſacrificed all his *activity* to *oſtentation*; and that he was encumbered by the pomp in which he placed his glory.

FABLE XXX.

The Fly in St. Paul's Cupola.

AS a Fly was crawling leifurely up one of the columns of St. Paul's Cupola, fhe often flopped, furveyed, examined, and at laft broke forth into the following exclamation. Strange! that any one who pretended to be an artift, fhould ever leave fo fuperb a ftructure, with fo many roughneffes unpolifhed! Ah, my friend! faid a very *learned architect*, who hung in his *web* under one of the capitals, you fhould never decide of things beyond the extent of your capacity. This lofty building was not erected for fuch diminutive animals as you or I; but for a certain fort of creatures, who are at leaft ten thoufand times as large: to their eyes, it is very poffible, thefe columns may feem as fmooth, as to you appear the wings of your favourite Miftrefs.

FABLE XXXI.

The Elm-tree and the Vine.

AN extravagant young Vine, vainly ambitious of independency, and fond of rambling at large, defpifed the alliance of a ftately Elm that grew near, and courted her embraces. Having

rifen

rifen to fome fmall height without any kind of fupport, fhe fhot forth her flimfey branches to a very uncommon and fuperfluous length; calling on her neighbour to take notice how little fhe wanted his affiftance. Poor infatuated fhrub, replied the Elm, how inconfiftent is thy conduct! Would'ft thou be *truly* independent, thou fhould'ft carefully apply thofe juices to the enlargement of thy ftem, which thou lavifheft in vain upon unne-ceffary foliage. I fhortly fhall behold thee grove-ling on the ground; yet countenanced, indeed, by many of the *human* race, who, intoxicated with vanity, have defpifed œconomy; and who, to fupport for a moment their empty boaft of in-dependence, have exhaufted the very *fource* of it in frivolous expences.

F A B L E XXXII.

The Laurustinus and the Rose-tree.

IN the quarters of a fhrubbery, where decidu-ous plants and ever-greens were intermingled with an air of negligence, it happened that a Rofe grew not far from a Laurustinus. The Rofe, enlivened by the breath of *June*, and attired in all its gorgeous bloffoms, looked with much con-tempt on the Laurustinus; who had nothing to difplay but the dufky verdure of its leaves. What

a

a wretched neighbourhood. cryed she, is this! and how unworthy to partake the honour of my company! Better to bloom and die in the defert, than to affociate myfelf here with fuch low and dirty vegetables. And is this my lot at laft, whom every nation has agreed to honour, and every Poet confpired to reverence, as the undoubted fovereign of the field and garden? If I really *am* fo, let my fubjects, at leaft, keep their diftance, and let a circle remain vacant round me, fuitable to the ftate my rank requires. Here, Gardiner, bring thy hatchet; prithee cut down this Lauruftinus; or at leaft remove it to its proper fphere. Be pacified, my lovely Rofe, replied the Gardiner; enjoy thy *fovereignty* with moderation, and thou fhalt receive all the homage which thy beauty can require. But remember that in winter, when neither thou nor any of thy tribe produce one flower or leaf to chear me, this faithful fhrub, which thou defpifeft. will become the glory of my garden. Prudence therefore, as well as gratitude, is concerned, in the protection of a friend, that will fhew his *Friendfhip in adverfity.*

M

FABLE

FABLE XXXIII.

The Senfitive Plant and the Palm-tree.

THE Senfitive Plant being brought out of the greenhoufe on a fine fummer's day, and placed in a beautiful grove, adorned with the fineſt foreſt trees and the moſt curious plants, began to give himfelf great airs, and to treat all that were about him with much petulance and difdain. Lord! fays fhe, how could the Gardiner think of fetting me among a parcel of Trees; grofs, inanimate things, mere vegetables, and perfect ſtocks! Sure he does not take *me* for a common plant, when he knows, that I have the fenfe of feeling in a more exquifite degree than he has himfelf. It really fhocks me to fee into what wretched low company he has introduced me: 'tis more than the delicacy of my conſtitution, and the extreme tendernefs of my nerves, can bear. Pray, Mrs. Acacia, ſtand a little farther off, and don't perfume quite fo much upon your idle pretence of being my coufin. Good Mr. Citron, keep your diſtance, I befeech you; your ſtrong fcent quite overpowers me. Friend Palm-tree, your offenfive fhade is really more than I am able to fupport. The lofty Palm-tree, tho' little moved by fo unmannerly an attack,

condefcended

condefcended to rebuke the impertinent creature
in the following manner. Thou vegetable frib-
ble! Learn to know thyfelf, and thy own worth-
leffnefs and infignificancy. Thou valueft thyfelf
on a vicious foftnefs, a falfe delicacy, the very
defect and imbecility of thy nature. What art
thou good for, that fhrinkeft at a touch, and
droopeft at a breath of air; feeble and barren,
a perpetual torment to thyfelf, and wholly ufelefs to others. Whereas we, whom thou treat-
eft with fuch difdain, make a grateful return to
man for his care of us: fome of us yield him fruit;
others are ferviceable to him by their ftrength
and firmnefs; we fhade him from the heat of the
fun, and we defend him from the violence of the
winds. I am particularly diftinguifhed for my
hardinefs and perfeverance, my fteadinefs and
conftancy: and on account of thofe very qualities which thou wanteft and affecteft to defpife,
have the honour to be made the emblem of con-
queft, and the reward of the Conqueror.

F A B L E XXXIV.

The Tentyrites and the Ichneumon.

A Crocodile of prodigious fize, and uncommon fiercenefs, infefted the banks of the
Nile, and fpread defolation through all the neigh-

                    bouring

bouring country. He seized the shepherd together with the sheep, and devoured the herdsman as well as the cattle. Emboldened by success, and the terror which prevailed wherever he appeared, he ventured to carry his incursions even into the island of Tentyra, and to brave the people, who boast themselves the only tamers of his race. The Tentyrites themselves were struck with horror, at the appearance of a monster so much more terrible than they had ever seen before: even the boldest of them dared not to attack him openly; and the most experienced long endeavoured with all their art and address to surprise him, but in vain. As they were consulting together, what they should do in these circumstances, an Ichneumon stepped forth, and thus addressed them. I perceive your destress, neighbours: and tho' I cannot assist you in the present difficulty, yet give me leave to offer you some advice that may be of use to you for the future. A little prudence is worth all your art and your courage: it may be glorious to overcome a great evil, but the wisest way is to prevent it. You despise the Crocodile while he is small and weak; and do not sufficiently consider, that, as he is a long-lived animal, so 'tis his peculiar property to grow as long as he lives. You see I am a poor, little, feeble creature; yet am I

much

much more terrible to the Crocodile, and more useful to the country, than you are. I attack him in the egg; and while you are contriving for months together, how to get the better of one Crocodile, and all to no purpose, I effectually destroy fifty of them in a day.

FABLE XXXV.

The Tulip and the Rose.

A Tulip and a Rose happened to be near neighbours in the same garden. They were *both* indeed extremely beautiful; yet the Rose engaged considerably more than an equal share of the gardiner's attention. Enamoured, as in truth he was, of the delicious odour it diffused; he appeared, in the eye of the Tulip to be always kissing and caressing it. The envy and jealousy of rival beauties are not easily to be concealed. The Tulip, vain of its external charms, and unable to bear the thought of being forsaken for another, remonstrated in these words against the Gardiner's partiality. Why are my beauties thus neglected? Are not my colours more bright, more various, and more inviting, than any which that red-faced Thing has to display? Why then is *she* to engross your whole affection, and thus for ever to be preferred?—Be not dissatisfied,

my

my fair Tulip, said the Gardiner, I acknowledge thy beauties, and admire them as they deserve. But there are found in my favourite Rose such attractive odours, such *internal* charms, that I enjoy a banquet in their fragrance, which no *mere* beauty can pretend to furnish.

F A B L E   XXXVI.

The Woodcock and the Mallard.

A Woodcock and a Mallard were feeding to-gether in some marshy ground at the tail of a mill-pond. Lard, says the squeamish Woodcock, in what a voracious and beastly manner do you devour all that comes before you! Neither snail, frog, toad, nor any kind of filth, can escape the fury of your enormous appetite. All alike goes down, without *measure* and without *distinction.*—What an odious vice is *Gluttony!*

Good-lack! Replied the Mallard, pray how came *you* to be my accuser? And whence has your excessive delicacy a right to censure my plain eating? Is it a crime to satisfy one's hunger? Or is it not indeed a *Virtue* rather, to be pleased with the food which nature offers us? Surely I would sooner be charged with gluttony, than with that finical and sickly appetite, on which *you* are

pleased

25 Love and Folly.

26 The Eclipse?

27 The Boy and ẏ Butterfly.

28 The Toad & the Ephemeron.

29 The Peacock.

30 The Fly in St. Paul's Cupola.

31 The Elm-tree and the Vine.

32 The Laurustinus & the Rose tree.

33 The Sentitive Plant & Palm tree.

34 The Sentinites & ẏ Ichneumon.

35 The Tulip & the Rose.

36 The Woodcock and Mallard.

pleafed to ground your fuperiority of *tafte.*—
What a filly vice is *Daintinefs.*

Thus endeavouring to palliate their refpective
paffions, our epicures parted with a mutual contempt. The Mallard hafting to devour fome gar-
bage, which was in reality a *bait,* immediately
gorged an hook thro' mere greedinefs and over-
fight: while the Woodcock, flying thro' a glade,
in order to feek his favourite juices, was entangled in a net, fpread acrofs it for that purpofe: falling each of them a facrifice to their
different, but *equal,* foibles.

F A B L E   XXXVII.

The two Trouts and the Gudgeon.

A Fifherman, in the month of May, ftood an-
gling on the banks of Thames, with an
artificial fly. He threw his bait with fo much
art, that a young Trout was rufhing towards it,
when fhe was prevented by her mother. Never,
faid fhe, my child, be too precipitate, where
there is a poffibility of danger. Take due time
to confider, before you rifk an action that *may* be
fatal. How know you whether yon appearance
be *indeed* a fly, or the fnare of an enemy?—Let
fome one elfe make the experiment *before* you.

If it *be* a fly, he very probably will elude the firft attack: and then the fecond may be made, if not with fuccefs, at leaft with fafety.—She had no fooner uttered this caution, than a Gudgeon feized upon the pretended fly, and became an example to the giddy daughter, of the great importance of her mother's counfel.

FABLE XXXVIII.

The Stars and the Sky-Rocket.

AS a Rocket, on a rejoicing night, afcended thro' the air, and obferved the ftream of light that diftinguifhed his paffage, he could not forbear exulting in his elevation, and calling upon the Stars to do him reverence. Behold, faid he, what gazing multitudes admire the luftre of *my* train, whilft all *your* feeble fparks of light pafs unobferved, or difregarded! The Stars heard his empty boaft with a filent indignation: the Dog-Star only vouchfafed to anfwer him. How weak are they, faid he, who value themfeves on the voice of popular applaufe! 'Tis true, the novelty of thy appearance may procure to *thee* more admiration than is allotted to *our* daily courfe, although indeed a lafting miracle. But do not eftimate thy importance by the capricious fancy of ill-judging mortals. Know thyfelf to be

the

the useless pageant, the frail production of a mortal hand. Even while I speak, thy blaze is extinguished, and thou art sunk into oblivion. We, on the other hand, were lighted up by heaven, for the advantage of mankind; and our glory shall endure for ever.

FABLE XXXIX.

The Farmer and his three Enemies.

A Wolf, a Fox, and a Hare, happened one evening to be foraging in different parts of a Farmer's yard. Their first effort was pretty successful, and they returned in safety to their several quarters: however not so happy, as to be unperceived by the Farmer's watchful eye; who, placing several kinds of snares, made each of them his prisoner in the next attempt. He first took the Hare to talk, who confessed she had eaten a few turnip-tops, merely to satisfy her hunger: besought him piteously to spare her life, and promised never to enter his grounds again. He then accosted the Fox; who in a fawning obsequious tone, protested, that he came into his premises, thro' no other motive, than pure good-will, to restrain the Hares and other vermin from the plunder of his corn; and that, whatever evil tongues might say, he had too great a regard,

both

both for him and for juftice, to be in the leaft capable of any difhoneft action.   He laft of all examined the Wolf, what bufinefs brought *him* within the purlieus of a Farmer's yard. The Wolf very impudently declared, it was with a view of deftroying his lambs, to which he had an undoubted right: that the Farmer himfelf was the only felon, who robbed the community of Wolves of what was meant to be their proper food. That this, at leaft, was his opinion: and whatever fate attended him, he fhould not fcruple to rifque his life in the purfuit of his lawful prey.

The Farmer having heard their pleas, determined the caufe in the following manner. The Hare, faid he, deferves compaffion, for the penitence he fhews, and the humble confeffion he has made:——As for the Fox and Wolf, let *them* be hanged *together;* their crimes themfelves *alike* deferve it, and are *equally* heightened by the aggravations of *hypocrify* and of *impudence.*

FABLE

FABLE XL.

The Snail and the Statue.

A Statue of the *Medicean* Venus was erected in a grove, sacred to beauty and the fine arts. Its modest attitude, its elegant proportions, affisted by the situation in which it was placed, attrackted the regard of every delicate observer.—— A Snail, who had fixed himself beneath the moulding of the pedestal, beheld with an evil eye the admiration it excited. Accordingly, watching his opportunity, he strove, by trailing his filthy slime over every limb and feature, to obliterate those beauties which he could not endure to hear so much applauded. An honest Linnet, however, who observed him at his dirty work, took the freedom to assure him, that he would infallibly lose his labour: For although, said he, to an injudicious eye, thou mayest fully the perfections of this finished piece, yet a more accurate and close inspector, will discover its beauty, thro' all the blemishes with which thou hast endeavoured to disguise it.

FABLE XLI.

The Water-fall.

FROM the head of a narrow valley that is wholly overshaded by the growth of trees, a large Cascade bursts forth with a luxuriance unexpected. First the current rushes down a precipice with headlong impetuosity; then dashed from rock to rock, and divided as it rolls along by fragments of stones or trunks of trees, it assumes a milk-white appearance, and sparkles thro' the gloom. All is intricacy; all is profusion: and the tide, however ample, appears yet *more* considerable by the fantastic growth of roots that hide the limits of its channel. Thus bounding down from one descent to another, it no sooner gains the level, than it sinks beneath the earth, and buries all its glory at our feet.

A spectator, privy to the scanty source which furnished out this grand appearance, stood one day in a musing posture, and began to moralize on its prodigality. Ah silly stream! said he, why wilt thou hasten to exhaust thy source, and thus wilfully incur the contempt that waits on poverty? Art thou ignorant that thy funds are by no means equal to this expence? Fear not, my kind

adviser,

advifer, replied the generous Cafcade; the gratitude I owe my mafter, who collected my rills into a ftream, induces me to entertain his friends in the beft manner I am able: when *alone*, I act with more œconomy.

FABLE XLII.

The Oak and the Sycamore.

A Sycamore grew befide an Oak; and being not a little elevated by the firft warm days in fpring, began to fhoot forth his leaves apace, and to defpife the naked Oak for *infenfibility*, and *want of fpirit*. The Oak, confcious of its fuperior nature, made this philofophical reply. Be not, my friend, fo much delighted with the firft addrefs of every fickle zephyr: confider the frofts may yet return: and if thou coveteft an equal fhare with me in all the glories of the rifing year, do not afford them an opportunity to nip thy beauties in their bud. As for myfelf, I only wait to fee this genial warmth a little confirmed: and, whenever this is the cafe, I fhall perhaps difplay a majefty that will not eafily be fhaken. But the tree that appears too fuddenly affected by the firft favourable glance of fpring, will ever be the firft to fhed its verdure. and to drop beneath the frowns of winter.

FABLE

FABLE XLIII.

The Wolf and the Shepherd's Dog.

A Wolf ranging over the foreſt, came within the borders of a ſheep-walk; when meeting with the Shepherd's Dog, that with a ſurly ſort of growl, demanded his buſineſs there, he thought proper to put on as innocent an appearance as he *could*, and proteſted upon his *honour*, that he meant not the leaſt offence. I am afraid, ſaid the Dog, the pledge of your *honour* is but a poor depoſite for your *honeſty:* you muſt not take it amiſs, if I object to the *Security*. No ſlur upon my reputation, replied the Wolf, I beg of you. My ſenſe of honour is as delicate, as my great atchievements are renowned. I would not leave a ſtain upon my memory for the world. The fame of what are commonly called *great atchieve-ments* is very precious, to be ſure, returned the Dog; almoſt equal to the character of an excellent butcher, a gallant highwayman, or an expert aſſaſſin. While the Dog was yet ſpeaking, a lamb happened to ſtray within reach of our hero. The temptation was ſtronger than he was able to reſiſt: He ſprung upon his prey, and was ſcouring haſtily away with it. However, the Dog ſeized and held him, till the arrival of the

Shepherd,

Shepherd, who took meafures for his execution. Juft as he was going to difpatch him; I obferve, fays the Dog, that one of your noble *atchieve-ments*, is the deftruction of the innocent. You are welcome to the renown, as you are alfo to the re-ward of it. As for me, I fhall prefer the credit of having *honeftly defended* my mafter's property, to any fame you have acquired by thus *heroically invading* it.

FABLE XLIV.

The Mufhroom and the Acorn.

AN Acorn fell from the top of an old vener-able Oak, full on the head of a Mufhroom that unhappily fprung up beneath it. Wounded by the blow, the Mufhroom complained of the incivility. Impertinent upftart, replied the Acorn, why didft thou, with familiar boldnefs, approach fo near to thy fuperiors? fhall the wretched off-fpring of a dunghill prefume to raife its head, on a fpot *ennobled* by my anceftors for fo many generations? I do not mean, returned the Mufh-room, to difpute the honour of thy birth, or to put my own in competition with it. On the contrary, I muft acknowledge that I hardly know from *whence* I fprung. But fure 'tis *merit*, and not mere anceftry, that obtains the regard of thofe,

whofe

whofe approbation is truly valuable : I have *little* perhaps to boaft, but furely thou who haft thus infulted me, canft have no pretence to boaft *any.* I pleafe the palates of mankind, and give a poignant flavour to their moft elegant entertainments; while thou, with all the pride of thy anceftry, art fit only to fatten Hogs.

FABLE XLV.

Wifdom and Selfifhnefs.

AS *Wifdom,* in the form of a beautiful young lady, was travelling along the road, it happened on a time, that fhe was benighted and loft her way. She had not however wandered far, when perceiving a light glimmer from a window at fome diftance, fhe endeavoured to direct her fteps towards the houfe where it appeared. This proved to be no other, than the miferable abode of *Selfifhnefs;* who, beneath the femblance of a churlifh and clofe-fifted peafant, had long taken up his refidence in this lonefome habitation. She knocked at the door, to enquire her way. The Lout opened it with caution; but, being immediately ftruck with the uncommon luftre of fo fine a figure, he found his appetite awake, and became impatient for the gratification of it. *Wifdom,* on the other hand, feeling

an

an utter deteſtation for him, would have willingly withdrawn herſelf; but alas! it was too late. He [illegible] forced he was [illegible]p, unto whom ſhe never could be induced to ſhew any marks of natural affection. She would not even own him for her proper offspring; and he was put into the hands of *Dullneſs*, to be nurſed and educated at her diſcretion. As he arrived to years of maturity, he was known by the name of *Cunning*. Some faint reſemblance which he bore of his *Mother*, procured him a degree of reſpect among perſons of ſmall diſcernment; and he ſhewed ſomewhat of *her* addreſs in regard to the *means* by which he gained his ends; but he had ſo much of the *Father*, as never to extend his aims to any truly noble or ſocial atchievement.

F A B L E XLVI.

The Toad and the Gold-fiſh.

AS a Gold-fiſh, newly brought from the warm regions of the eaſt, diſplayed his beauties in the ſun; a Toad, who had long eyed him with no ſmall degree of envy, broke out into this exclamation. How partial and how fantaſtic is the favour of mankind! regardleſs of

every

every excellency that is obvious and familiar; and only ſtruck with what is imported form a diſtant climate at a large expence! What a pompous baſon is here conſtructed, and what extreme fondneſs is here ſhewn, for this inſignificant ſtranger! While a *quadrupede* of my importance is neglected, ſhunned, and even perſecuted. Surely were I to appear in China, I ſhould receive the fame, or perhaps greater honours, than are laviſhed here upon this tinſel favourite.

The Gold-fiſh, conſcious of his real beauty, and ſomewhat angry to be thus inſulted by ſo very unſightly and deformed a creature, made this rational reply. It muſt be confeſſed, that the opinions of men, are ſometimes guided by the caprice you mention. Yet, as for me and the reſt of my tribe, it is well known that if we are admired in England, we are not leſs admired at home: being there eſteemed by the greateſt mandarins, fed by ſtated officers, and lodged in baſons as ſuperb as any your nation has to boaſt. Perhaps then, notwithſtanding your ſage remark, there are ſome virtues and ſome qualities that pleaſe or diſguſt almoſt univerſally; and as *innocence* joined to *beauty* ſeldom fails to procure eſteem, ſo *malice* added to *deformity* will cauſe as general a deteſtation.

FABLE

FABLE XLVII.

The Hermit.

A Certain Hermit had fcooped his cave near the fummit of a lofty mountain, from whence he had an opportunity of furveying a large extent both of fea and land. He fate one evening, contemplating with pleafure on the objects that lay diffufed before him. The woods were dreft in the brighteft verdure; the thickets adorned with the gayeft bloffoms. The birds caroled beneath the branches; the lambs frolicked around the meads; the peafant whiftled befide his team; and the fhips driving by the gentle gales were returning fafely into their proper harbours. In fhort, the arrival of fpring had doubly enlivened the whole fcene before his eye; and every object yielded a difplay either of *beauty* or of *happinefs*.

On a fudden arofe a violent ftorm. The winds muftered all their fury, and whole forefts of oak lay fcattered on the ground. Darknefs inftantly fucceeded; hail-ftones and rain were poured forth in cataracts, and lightning and thunder added horror to the gloom.

N 2

And

And now the sea piled up in mountains bore aloft the largeſt veſſels; while the horrid uproar of its waves drowned the ſhrieks of the wretched mariners. When the whole tempeſt had exhauſted its fury, it was inſtantly followed by the ſhock of an earthquake.

The poor inhabitants of the beighbouring villages flocked in crowds to our Hermit's cave; religiouſly hoping, that his well-known ſanctity would be able to protect them in their diſtreſs. They were, however, not a little ſurpriſed at the profound tranquility that appeared in his countenance. "My friends, ſaid he, be not diſmayed. Terrible to *me*, as well as to *you*, would have been the war of elements we have juſt beheld; but that I have meditated with ſo much attention on the various works of Providence, as to be perſuaded that his *goodneſs* is equal to his *power*".

F A B L E XLVIII.

The Dove.

A Dove that had a mate and young ones, happening to ſpy her cage door open, was driven by a ſudden impulſe to fly out into an adjacent grove. There, perched upon the bough of a ſycamore, ſhe ſate as it were wrapt in deep contemplation;

templation; not recovering from her reverie, until the owner drew nigh unseen, and brought her back to her little family.

Art thou not afhamed then, fays her mate, thus to defert thy helplefs offspring? Art thou not bafe to abandon *me*, for the company of birds to whom thou art a ftranger? Could I have harboured fuch a thought? I, who have been ever conftant to our firft engagement; and muft have died of mere defpair, hadft thou not returned to my embraces? But how, alas, returned! Not, as it feems by choice; but enfnared by dint of artifice, and brought hither by conftraint.

Have patience, replied the rambler, and hear the plea of thy repentant mate. Witnefs all ye powers of wedlock, ye that know what paffes in the hearts of Doves, if ever, before this unhappy moment, I felt a wifh to part from thee! The door fo feldom open, allowed but one moment for deliberation, and I happened to decide amifs. When removed to yonder wood, the air of liberty breathed fo very fweet, that, with horror I fpeak it, I felt a fufpenfe about returning to the cage. Pardon, I pray thee, this one crime, and be well affured I will never repeat it. And that thou may'ft be the more induced to pardon

me,

me, know that the love of liberty burns ever the ftrongeft, in bofoms that are moft open to conjugal affection and the love of young.

FABLE XLIX.

The Nightingale and Bullfinch.

A Nightingale and a Bullfinch occupied two cages in the fame appartment. The Nightingale perpetually varied her fong, and every effort fhe made, afforded frefh entertainment. The Bullfinch always whiftled the fame dull tune that he had learnt, 'till all the family grew weary of the difguftful repetition. What is the reafon, faid the Bullfinch one day to his neighbour, that your fongs are always heard with peculiar attention, while mine, I obferve, are almoft as wholly difregarded? The reafon, replied the Nightingale, is obvious; your audience are fufficiently acquainted with every note you have been taught, and they know your natural abilities too well, to expect any thing new from *that quarter.* How then can you fuppofe they will liften to a fongfter, from whom nothing *native* or *original* is to be expected?

37. The Trouts
& the Gudgeon

38. The Stars &
the Sky-rocket.

39. The Farmer
& his Enemies.

40. The Snail
& the Statue.

41. The Water-
fall. —

42. The Oak &
the Sycamour

43. The Wolf &
Shepherd's Dog

44. The Mush-
room & the Acorn

45. Wisdom and
Cunning.

46. The Toad
& y Gold-fish.

47. The
Hermit. —

48. The Dove.

FABLE L.

The Fighting Cocks and the Turkey.

TWO Cocks of the genuine game-breed, met by chance upon the confines of their refpective walks. To fuch *great* and *heroic* fouls, the fmalleft matter imaginable affords occafion for difpute. They approached each other with pride and indignation; they looked defiance; they crow a challenge; and immediately commences a long and bloody battle. It was fought on both fides with fo much courage and dexterity; they gave and they received fuch deep and defperate wounds; that they both lay down upon the turf utterly fpent, blinded, and difabled. While this was their fituation, a Turkey that had been a fpectator of all that paffed between them, drew near to the field of battle, and reproved them in this manner. "How foolifh and abfurd has been your quarrel, my good neighbours! A more ridiculous one could fcarce have happened, amongft the moft contentious of all creatures, men. Becaufe you have crowed perhaps in each other's hearing, or one of you have picked up a grain of corn upon the territories of his rival, you have both rendered yourfelves miferable for the reminder of your days.

N 4

FABLE

FABLE LI.

The King-fisher and the Sparrow.

AS a King-fisher was fitting beneath the shade, upon the banks of a river; she was surprised on a sudden by the fluttering of a Sparrow, that had eloped from the neighbouring town, to visit her. When the first compliments were over, "How is it possible, said the Sparrow, that a bird so finely adorned, can think of spending all her days in the very depth of retirement ! The golden plumage of your breast, the shining azure of your pinions, were never given you to be concealed, but to attract the wonder of beholders. Why then should you not endeavour to know the world, and be, at the same time, yourself, both known and admired ?" You are very complaisant at least, replied the King-fisher, to conclude that my being *admired,* would be the consequence of my being *known.* But it has sometimes been my lot, in the lonesome valleys that I frequent, to hear the complaints of *beauty* that has been neglected; and of *worth* that has been despised. Possibly it does not always happen, that even *superior excellence* is found to excite admiration, or obtain encouragement. I have learned besides, not to build my happiness upon the opi-

nion

nion of others, so much as upon my own self-conviction, and the approbation of my own heart. Remember, I am a King-fisher; these woods and streams are my delight; and so long as they are free from winds and tempests, believe me, I am perfectly content with my situation. Why therefore should I court the noise and bustle of the world, which I find so little agreeable to my native disposition? It may be the joy of a Sparrow to indulge his curiosity, and to display his eloquence. I, for my part, love silence, privacy, and contemplation; and think that every-one should consult the native bias of his temper, before he chuses the way of life in which he expects to meet with happiness.

FABLE LII.

The Bee and the Spider.

ON the leaves and flowers of the same shrub, a Spider and a Bee pursued their several occupations; the one covering her thighs with honey; the other distending his bag with poison. The Spider, as he glanced his eye obliquely at the Bee, was ruminating with spleen on the superiority of her production. And how happens it, said he, in a peevish tone, that I am able to collect nothing but poison from the self-same plant,

plant, that fupplies *thee* with honey? My pains and induftry are not lefs than thine; in thofe refpects, we are each indefatigable. It proceeds only, replied the Bee, from the different difpofition of our nature: *mine* gives a pleafing flavour to every thing I touch; whereas *thine* converts it to poifon, what by a different procefs had been the pureft honey.

INDEX

49. The Nightingale & Bullfinch.
50. The Fighting Cocks & Turkeys.
51. The King-fisher & Sparrows.
52. The Bee & the Spider.

I N D E X.

F A B L E XVII.

The Wolf and the Crane.

'Tis the utmost extent of some men's gratitude, barely to refrain from oppressing and injuring their bene factors.

F A B L E XVIII.

The Country-man and the Snake.

To confer either power upon the mischievous, or favours on the undeserving, is a misapplication of our benevolence.

F A B L E XIX.

The Dog and the Shadow.

An over-greedy disposition often subjects us to lose what we already possess.

F A B L E XX.

The Sun and the Wind.

Gentle means, on many occasions, are more effectual than violent ones.

F A B L E XXI.

The Wolf and the Mastiff.

A mere competence with liberty, is preferable to servitude amid the greatest affluence.

F A B L E XXII.

Fortune and the School-boy.

We are always ready to censure fortune for the ill effects of our own carelessness.

I N D E X.

I N D E X.

O 4

I N D E X.

INDEX

TO THE

THIRD BOOK.

I N D E X.

I N D E X.

I N D E X.

P 2

I N D E X.

FINIS.

www.ingramcontent.com/pod-product-compliance
Lightning Source LLC
Chambersburg PA
CBHW031021120726
47905CB00007B/2000